About the Author

Mark Vaughn is the author of *The Honey Tree* and *The Torch: The Annie Moore Story*. He is the son of a minister and the grandson of a Pearl Harbor survivor. His grandparents emigrated from Denmark to the United States through Canada. He is the father of two children and has worked as a minister and physician assistant.

Oils of Arizona

Mark Vaughn

Oils of Arizona

Olympia Publishers

London

www.olympiapublishers.com
OLYMPIA PAPERBACK EDITION

Copyright © Mark Vaughn 2024

The right of Mark Vaughn to be identified as author of
this work has been asserted in accordance with sections 77 and 78
of the Copyright, Designs and Patents Act 1988.

All Rights Reserved

No reproduction, copy or transmission of this publication
may be made without written permission.
No paragraph of this publication may be reproduced,
copied or transmitted save with the written permission of the
publisher, or in accordance with the provisions
of the Copyright Act 1956 (as amended).

Any person who commits any unauthorised act in relation to
this publication may be liable to criminal
prosecution and civil claims for damage.

A CIP catalogue record for this title is
available from the British Library.

ISBN: 978-1-80074-196-6

This is a work of fiction.
Names, characters, places and incidents originate from the writer's
imagination. Any resemblance to actual persons, living or dead, is
purely coincidental.

First Published in 2024

Olympia Publishers
Tallis House
2 Tallis Street
London
EC4Y 0AB

Printed in Great Britain

Dedication

To my grandparents, Albert and Eleanor Vaughn, and Bill and Marion McIntyre.

Acknowledgments

The First United African Methodist Church in Athens, Ga., the University of Georgia, and the Hillsborough County Public Libraries.

Book One
Black Pearls

Pearls
Standing on a mountain peak
A Samurai path to comfort me
Roads that lead to the sea
And there beside an emerald bay
Divers dive for pearls
On most any day
One day, those divers looked at me
They said
Come and see
And it was there
I discovered me.

Ecclesiastes 13:44-45 "Vanity, Vanity all is vanity says the teacher, a chasing after the wind."

Matthew 13: 44-45 "The Kingdom of Heaven is like a treasure buried in a field, that a man found in a field, and then reburied. Then in his joy goes and sells everything he has and buys that field.
And the Kingdom of heaven is like a merchant in search of fine pearls. When he found one priceless pearl, he went and sold everything that he had and bought it."

"In the long history of the world, only a few generations have been granted the role of defending freedom in its hour of maximum danger. I do not shrink from this responsibility—I welcome it. I do not believe that any of us would exchange places with any other people or any other generation. The energy, the faith, the devotion which we bring to this endeavor will light our country and all who serve it, and the glow from that fire can truly light the world.

And so, my fellow Americans: ask not what your country can do for you, ask what you can do for your country.

My fellow citizens of the world: ask not what America will do for you, but what together we can do for the freedom of man.

Finally, whether you are citizens of America or citizens of the world, ask of us here the same high standards of strength and sacrifice which we ask of you. With a good conscience our only sure reward, with history the final judge of our deeds, let us go forth to lead the land we love, asking His blessing and His help, but knowing that here on earth God's work must truly be our own."

- John F Kennedy's inaugural speech on 20 Jan 1961 (http://www.presidency.ucsb.edu/ws/index.php?pid=8032&)

Chapter One
The Wind

The newspaper headlines had read that morning, '*Mississippi Jails Freedom Riders.*' An article under it also on the front page read, '*Arrested Riders Now At 110.*' But they were not the headlines that Sammy von Burger read. His interest was in the sports section. He looked at the box score for the Cubbies on his way to ball practice.

The stadium for the games was nothing more than a glorified little league field with a chain link fence. There was a roof over the dug-outs, and a step-down onto a concrete floor, with sparsely scattered sand from the bottom of cleats. Behind the fence was a grove of oaks framing a set of wooden benches with seating for a couple of hundred fans. All in all, Panther Stadium could have passed for a low-scale minor league field.

As usual, Sammy and Robert arrived early to the park. They did their usual stretches and then began their warm-up tosses. Sammy was a senior that year and the game that day would be the last of the year. It was just a few weeks before his graduation. He was seventeen, young for a senior. He wouldn't be eighteen until graduation on July 15.

Like all eighteen-year-olds, he would then sign up for selective service. There were always rumblings abroad, but in the tenuous peace, the last thing on Robert and Sammy's minds was being drafted. Two years of servitude in any of the branches of the military seemed out of the question for Samuel, "Sammy" von Burger; the eldest child of Jon and Chloe von Burger.

He had been born in 1945. After his dad took a brief post in Chicago, he then joined the Chicago Police Department. His mom and dad had migrated from Germany in the late 1930s about the time John Steinbeck was penning *The Grapes of Wrath*. His dad earned his citizenship through his distinguished military service. His mother acquired naturalized citizenship. His dad said his mom got her citizenship because she was 'such a good gal,' whereas he had to earn his.

His dad's best friend was a Jewish man named Samuel Gillespie, and his mom and dad helped his family escape the beginnings of tyranny in Europe. Many Jews suffered in the Holocaust that took place, but not Samuel. He even liked German Fraulein's. He seemed to have a weakness for them, marrying not just one, but two.

Sammy did not share his father's view of life and discipline, but was generally a good kid. He had a rebellious streak and didn't care for a lot of rules, but he stayed out of trouble, and that meant something.

Sammy's dad wanted him to enlist in the navy. What Sammy hoped was to divert to a more radical Peace Corp that the newly elected president had as a part of his platform. It usually wasn't convenient for Sammy to pay attention to politics, but for once Sammy and his dad agreed. They both thought the election of John F Kennedy was the best thing since canned beer. Sammy only drank one when he could get away with it, but he appreciated the can.

But for now, in May 1961, Sammy would settle for graduating and then dreaming about tomorrow with beautiful Bonnie "B." Her full name was Bonnie Ruth Becker, and she was the daughter of an army officer.

"I heard Jackie Robinson voted for Richard Nixon," said Sammy as he threw a lob to Robert.

Robert ran up and fielded the pop fly. Bobby Butler was destined for greatness. He had broken the all-time high school record in the state of Illinois for runs batted in. He had kept a batting average of 400, and hit 20 home runs. He had an eye that wouldn't quit. It wasn't like they had a pitiful schedule; they played the team that won the district last year twice. They were going to win it again, and this was it for all of them. Everyone thought with the scouts that had been rumored to be at the games, Bobby might go in the draft.

"Where'd you hear that?" responded Bobby as he took a toss and then threw it back.

"I saw it in the *Chicago Tribune*. It said he wrote a letter to President Kennedy congratulating him, but saying he would have preferred it if Richard Nixon would have won," said Sammy. He slung the ball…

"Don't take it out on me, man," said Bobby. "Really? Huh? He still your hero?"

Sammy slung another fast ball.

"Well, what did the letter say?" asked Bobby.

"He wasn't talking baseball, that's for sure," said Sammy. "It was the usual boring political drivel."

Bobby laughed. "Yeah, you got a C minus in civics—Ahhh!"

"That was a B minus, thank you very much," said Sammy. "Wasn't it you who got the C?"

"I'm a baseball player, not a politician."

"That's what they all say," said Sammy.

"They ALL don't hit the baseball like I do," said Bobby.

"So, if it was you, and you were say, like, a Jackie Robinson, what would you have written?" asked Sammy.

"I'd have told John F Kennedy his wife deserved a lover like me," said Bobby.

This caused some laughter from the other players who were beginning to show up and stretch.

"No shit," said Sammy.

"I'm a lover, not a politician," said Bobby.

"I thought you said you were a baseball player," said Ruben, a tall pitcher on the team who had a good curve ball and changeup, but was the losing pitcher on record in their loss to their cross-town rival, the district champion.

"That I am," said Bobby. "How 'bout you?"

There was more general laughter.

"I'd settle for lover if I could be with a chick like the First Lady."

"Did Bonnie see the letter? She got an A in civics and everything else," said Bobby.

"Her dad is nearly a general," said another teammate. "She's supposed to be smart."

"He ain't a general," said Sammy. "I think he's a colonel."

"Pretty good for a darkie, huh," said Bobby. "You know if I was white, I wouldn't be a very good lover."

"What about baseball player?" asked Reuben.

"You're white, you tell me," said Bobby. Rueben wasn't completely white, but mixed Caucasian. But he took the jab in good fun.

"What do you think she said?" said Sammy.

"She towed the party line, guess who her father voted for," said Sammy.

"You sure you ain't black and she's white? She's black, ain't she?" said Bobby.

"You're full of shit," said Sammy.

"Jackie Robinson is a republican," said Bobby loud enough for the entire field of players to hear. He then whispered Sammy's way, "Does the crinkled nose trick still work with Bonnie B?"

"Let's go, boys..." said the coach in the dugout.

"You bastard," said Sammy as he headed toward the dugout.

"Better be careful, it might make you vote republican," said Bobby. "Ahhh!"

"Bobby!" said the coach. "Think about baseball for a change. You're on clean up."

It was May 15, 1961. Three weeks from graduation. As Sammy turned his head, he saw Bonnie take a seat. He waved. Beautiful Bonnie B. He supposed he could be a republican for her... after John F Kennedy was president. He might even enlist in the navy for her.

Chapter Two
Captain Becker and Jackie Robinson

The date started out well enough. And then it all went downhill from there. When Sammy knocked over his iced tea, and it spilled all over Bonnie, the evening was almost over. Sammy talked her into changing into more comfortable clothes, then talked her into a walk by Lake Michigan. They were at an expensive shin-dig downtown, so it wasn't a long drive. The 'more comfortable clothes' cost him. Good thing he had bought gas the night before. As they arrived, it seemed all had been forgiven. The moon was rising, the sun setting… when their argument began again.

"What is wrong with you tonight?" asked Sammy, arms in the air, settling to prop on his waist. He looked like his third base coach from school. "You've been irritable all day long, and what does this have to do with Jackie Robinson?"

Bonnie shot him a defensive glance. Hand holding was put on hold for the rest of the night. There would be absolutely no necking.

Sammy went on, looking away as if speaking to someone far off sitting on the full moon over head.

"You always bring up Jackie Robinson. He just so happens to be my childhood hero, the one I am trying to be like… only, I'm white."

"Exactly," said Bonnie.

It was quiet. Bonnie was a beautiful black woman, she could be a model in any popular fashion magazine.

"It's baseball... and haven't I shown respect? Haven't I asked for your hand? Do you think I don't love you?" asked Sammy.

"You don't want my hand, Sammy von Burger. Everyone knows what you want... and I AM a baseball fan, I know what it means. But I am a bigger fan of High School Baseball than the Majors, and who was it that didn't miss a single game?" replied Bonnie.

This had been an ongoing argument that had festered over the last few months; Sammy's last season. Sammy was quite good, and had hopes of being drafted to a farm club. Finally, with a sly smile, Sammy answered, "Bobby?"

"Sammy!" Bonnie headed away from the car and apparently without a course, a path to nowhere, blind with rage at something unsaid.

"I'm sorry!" said Sammy. " I was trying to be funny... bad joke. You always say you wish I was more like him, and then you say you wish I was more like your old man."

Bonnie finally realized she had no destination and stopped and faced Sammy. Finally, she spoke what was unsaid, "I'm pregnant." Then she began to sob.

Sammy was too shell shocked to respond well, but he finally took Bonnie in his arms. Hid old man always told him that this could happen if...

Trying to be his best Jackie Robinson, he asked her, "How long have you been pregnant?" It did not sound like Jackie Robinson, or her old man, or his old man for that matter, but an awful lot like a scared and shell-shocked Sammy. Under his breath, he made the mistake of uttering one phrase that set off Bonnie again. "Whoa" is what he said.

Finally, she calmed down, and they both sat down. Sammy wanted to cry, but didn't; Bonnie cried enough for both of them.

"Yes, you have loved me, but what are we going to do? I haven't told Daddy yet. But I think he already knows, and Momma is fit to be tied. And don't you say one word about Sallie Mae Cowert."

Sammy sighed. "I wasn't going to mention her. Whoa!" he said again... and both sat silently for a moment.

"I guess that's why I am mad about baseball now. Sammy, we're gonna have a baby... you can't afford to play baseball," said Bonnie.

"Oh man," was all that Sammy could come up with. His dreams of running on to a major league ball field were going up in smoke. Sammy had, despite his rebellious nature, always been a responsible man. But on the horizon were storm clouds for things other than his baseball career. There were advisors being sent to Vietnam. There were murmurings of war.

Now he understood what Bonnie was talking about. Her father had enlisted at a young age. Her momma swore to Bonnie that she didn't want her daughter to make the same mistakes she did. Now that was a can of worms to open. It was always good when Captain Becker would ask Sammy to see his medals in the den, when the two of them started up.

"You're not even black," said Bonnie.

Sammy again was dumbfounded. "It was never a problem before. What was it you were saying about my white ass?"

Bonnie started giggling. "I'm sorry, Sammy... Sammy, what do you want me to do? We could get married."

Sammy's face suddenly went pale with the prospects of responsibility now upon him. But he was not so different from other males his age who had registered for the selective service. Marriage when facing the draft was not such a bad option.

"Marriage?" said Sammy.

"You don't want to marry me?" she asked. "I can't get an abortion, my daddy would kill me. You heard what happened to Sandra."

Sammy's face turned an even whiter shade of pale. "*Ugh!*" was what he inaudibly exclaimed inside. No matter the date had gone from good to worse in a matter of minutes. The spilled tea probably did cool things down.

But reality was better than blind ignorance, and fantasies of a baseball career that was iffy at best. He just wasn't ready to grow up. Captain Becker and his dad had told him stories of war. The adventure -when a possibility suddenly paled worse than the color of his face .

"I guess I'll tell my family. Maybe Mom could break the news to Dad gently."

Bonnie giggled again. "Sammy, will you marry me?" she finally asked.

"Yeah, Bonnie, I will," said Sammy.

They got in the car and he drove her home. He kissed her passionately on her porch. The light went off as usual when they had kissed too long.

For a fairly bad night out with Bonnie Becker, it sure ended well.

Chapter Three
Graduation

Everyone in the gymnasium was standing, some with their hands over their hearts, as the high school band played the star-spangled banner. One family remained seated, everyone knew why; they were Jehovah's Witness. As the band played, a few sang the anthem quietly. At the conclusion, a black minister from a local Baptist congregation said a prayer.

There was some fidgeting among the graduates as the honor students spoke. Then the principal, a brother to the minster, began the commencement. As Sammy received his diploma, he gave a slight wave to his mom. Chloe gave a quick wave and a smile. Then after a long parade of students, and a few encouraging words, caps flew into the air, and cheers were all around.

"OK, smile!" said Chloe as she held her camera. It was a new one with twenty exposures or so, and a cube flash. They were still in the gymnasium, where the graduation had just taken place. Sammy was doing everything to look like he was appreciative to his mother for displaying him in front of his whole school in such a way. He was on the platform holding his diploma.

Students were scattered across the gymnasium floor, and

out into the yard. There was a light cacophony of conversation, as the ambience of pomp and circumstance ended in this dinumeaux.

Bonnie B laughed at Sammy's discomfort, and hopped up onto the platform with him. He finally relaxed a little and posed with her. Snap, bright light, red stars, and another picture. One thing Sammy understood about his mother was that she loved to take pictures. If she had been a newspaper reporter, she'd have won the Pulitzer by now.

Bobby walked from the back as Sammy descended the platform. A pretty blonde named Sarah was with him. How was it that he was with this black woman, who he was sure he would be with for the rest of his life, and Bobby, a black man, was with a blonde that looked like Marilyn Monroe? It must have had something to do with Samuel, the Jewish man who was his name sake, who loved a Fraulein. As Bobby and Sammy began to talk, their girls and Sammy's momma met up with Bobby's mom for a chat and some gossip. He supposed it was the kind of gossip you might have with tea and crumpets. He had had enough of those when he was younger. He and Bobby sat down.

Salt and pepper. Some said piss and vinegar, but that was a matter of opinion, and a matter of whether it was Sammy and Bobby, or Sarah and Bonnie.

"So, this is it. Doesn't seem real yet," said Bobby to Sammy.

"I'll come and see you when you report to camp for drills," said Sammy. Bobby had been drafted. Luckily, he had been drafted by two clubs, one run by Uncle Sam, no relation, and the other a team with major league potential.

"You going to enlist?" asked Bobby.

"I don't know, man," said Sammy.

"You know what I told you, you wait on them and they will put you where they want to. You enlist, you at least have some say," said Bobby.

"You think there will be another war?"

Bobby just looked at him.

"Yeah, I think so too. Dad never says anything when the news is on anymore," said Sammy.

"Cheer up, man, it's graduation!" said Bobby.

"You coming over to my place later?" asked Sammy.

"As long as you tell the guy with the gun I'm not Superman," said Bobby.

Sammy laughed. "That old coot; that's his way of saying welcome to the neighborhood. He is an equal opportunity harasser. Besides, I just graduated from a black school, against my father's wishes."

"I'll be there, dude," said Bobby.

"See you around, better get back," said Sammy.

Bobby nodded and caught up with Sarah, as Sammy put his arm around Bonnie.

The incident that led to Sammy being enrolled into Washington High School was not a pretty one. He had been at a Catholic School when he had differences with his teacher, and the nun in charge. He said words that caused him to be expelled, causing him great hardship with his father, who the whole city knew was a war hero. His dad said, "If that's the way you feel, then I will enroll you at Washington."

Sammy said, "Sure, Pops, sounds good to me." He had been grounded for a month, and he had thought it eternity, when, finally, his father lightened up.

His dad told him why he had come to the United States.

"That's really the reason?" Sammy had asked.

"Yeah," said Jon. "I'm not a prejudiced man, but I'm not a fool either."

Sammy had fallen in love with the beautiful Bonnie B, and she was pregnant. So, Jon thought the best thing to do was 'break Sammy in.' Then Bonnie had an abortion. It caused so much friction in the family that Chloe had become a Pentecostal. She would go down front and pray and speak in tongues. "Whatever it takes," she'd say.

Finally, Sammy had graduated. His dad was still mad at him, but was lightening up. He liked Bobby, he came to the games sometimes. Jon never was big on sports, but liked baseball. He always said he was a realist, a pragmatist, but was wild as all get out—and this was 1961.

The one thing Sammy hated the most was, "Jackie Robinson voted for Nixon!"

But graduation day had finally arrived. He got along with Col. Becker pretty well. He'd go to him for advice. Usually, he'd meet Bobby at the Beckers', or at Bobby's. It seemed he was more accepted in the black neighborhood than Bobby and Bonnie were in his. The whole neighborhood thought they were odd.

"Jon von Burger's a German immigrant and a war hero," they'd say. "A pragmatist, a realist, and a cop in Chicago."

Thank God for graduation. Maybe he would enlist.

Chapter Four
Uncle Sam and Sammy

"Hello, Mrs. Becker," said Jon von Burger.

He was in a suit and tie for this occasion. He preferred casual dress, and a T-shirt or no shirt around the house. He was greeted by a kind negro woman, well dressed and with impeccable manners. She was the wife of Captain Becker of the United States Army. She took great pride in this, for the history found in her family tree spoke of hard work and trials. Chloe related well to her. During the time Sammy had dated Bonnie, she had gotten to know Mrs. Becker well. She had also told them their immediate family history. She rarely spoke of their days at Pearl anymore, but with Mrs. Becker, Barbara, after a few cups of tea, she was able to speak openly about them. There was a kind of freedom in that for the two ladies.

At the time, Mrs. Becker was 'stationed' at the family house in Chicago, in a suburb just down the road from Sammy's high school. Bonnie and Sammy were said to have met in English class, but quickly learned to speak French. Actually, they met in homeroom, and except for Sally May Rogers, and a couple of other quick flings, there had been no one else for Sammy but Bonnie. He'd had a crush on her since the fifth grade.

Jon had come to call on Mrs. Becker to apologize and make amends for his son's indiscretions and immaturity. It was a job he was becoming very good at.

Mrs. Becker invited them into their living room and called for Bonnie. John had spoken on the phone with both Mrs. Becker and the captain, and had already apologized profusely. It was the first time he'd seen his first-born so contrite in quite some time. Jon even began to feel a little sorry for Sammy.

Bonnie walked in wearing Sammy's letterman sweater and had a seat, politely crossing her legs. Mrs. Becker had coffee ready. She knew Jon preferred coffee to tea as her husband did. A little boy poked his head around the corner and then quickly disappeared. With a word of warning from Mrs. Becker to the young boy, they all sat for coffee.

"That's my sister's youngest," said Barbara. "A well-behaved child, but curious like a cat."

They all sipped a little coffee, Bonnie nervously ate some cookies.

"I have telegraphed the captain after our conversation a few days ago. I told him as soon as we knew, and he has thanked you for your discretion regarding this and your call. We live on a captain's pay, so I didn't even try to reach him by phone. I found out from Bonnie before graduation, and I thought it was best to let graduation and the end of school pass before Bonnie told Sammy the news."

"I think you handled the situation just fine, Mrs. Becker," said Jon. He felt a bit like he was speaking to a superior. He was a bit on his heels as he did.

"Well," continued Mrs. Becker, who was a lady in every respect, "the captain and I went through something similar, only he was already in the army." Mrs. Becker had become pregnant with their first; presumably while the captain was on leave from boot camp. The difficulty and the humor of the situation was not lost on her. Sammy had been very free in his remarks about the military, as well as his lack of desire to go into the military. The option that all agreed upon to help quickly resolve the crisis was enlistment in the army. Mrs. Becker could even feel the laughter of her husband as she told him that Sammy had decided to 'join up.' Sammy even had what looked like a bit of civic pride in doing so. But Mr. von Burger had told her the rest of the story. Sammy had taken to moping around the house, and his baseball went limp on the shelves. "So, I'm going to be a grandfather" was all the captain would say.

"I think it shows good character for Sammy to act so responsibly," said Barbara.

"Sammy should be here soon," said Bonnie.

"Yes, I know, dear," said Barbara.

Almost as if on cue, a car turned off its ignition outside, and all watched while sipping coffee as Sammy quickly hopped across the lawn to the front door. Bonnie quickly stood to open the door. Sparks sometimes flew when those two were around each other. It would be a shame if something happened to their relationship to change all this.

"You don't have to knock, come on in, Sammy," said Mrs. Becker.

"Yes, ma'am," said Sammy nervously as he caught his breath. He quickly fixed his hair and took a seat. As a general rule, Sammy had a difficult time understanding any adults except his mom. This special occasion was no different.

Mrs. Becker let him settle into his coffee. He sipped just a little loudly as it burnt his lips.

"Careful now" was all he heard.

"I know you all love Bonnie, you love her like we do," started Mrs. Becker.

"Well, we all thought the military would be a good option for them," said Jon.

Mrs. Becker gradually gathered her composure. "We owe a lot to the army. We would live a little harder if it hadn't opened doors for us as a couple." There was a picture of the captain after OCS. She looked up at it, it was over the mantle. It seemed to be who the Beckers were as family. "He got into OCS just after the Presidential Order."

"Yeah, I voted for Truman. I always try to vote for a winner," said Jon. He was what most called a 'Yellow Dog' Democrat with his politics now. Other than the responsibility of his oldest, Sammy was a chip off the old block. "Did you say they were sending your husband to Vietnam?"

"He's already there. Deployment is the downside of being a military wife."

Jon smiled. "Will your husband be attending the wedding?"

"He wouldn't miss it for the world—special deferment."

Jon smiled, Sammy fidgeted, and Bonnie glowed.

Chapter Five
Boot Camp

Pay phones weren't too hard to find on the road back from Paris Island.

"Momma, I just dropped him off," said Bonnie, stifling tears.

"You'll see him soon enough. Give him a chance to break in. Think about your wedding day," said Barbara Becker.

"OK, Momma."

"One rule the captain and I have regarding weddings is this: Sammy may visit up to the wedding day and one night before, but it's bad luck to see the bride before the wedding. This is like your own basic," said Mrs. Becker. She could see Bonnie smile through the telephone line.

"Yeah" was all she said.

"You come on home, now. I'll be giving Chloe von Burger a call. We'll go and look at invitations," said Mrs. Becker.

"I'm on my way."

The sun was hot. Thank God, it was going down. The first day of basic had been all that Sammy had expected. He felt absolutely humble, exhausted, and now was wondering how he was going to make it to the end. Tomorrow, they would be learning about the 'beautiful bitch,' an M-16 rifle. He had decided the Marines were the way to go. It would make him a man. He hadn't thrown up. But supper would be soon.

Finally, Sammy heaved over and puked.

"Ice Burger, isn't it?"

"No, sir, von Burger…"

"First day." The drill sergeant stifled a laugh. "I suppose I can take it easy on you, boy. You know how to peel potatoes?"

"Yes, sir," said Sammy from his knees.

"Go get cleaned up. Baseball ain't football, is it… Company dismissed."

A group of new recruits with shaved heads looked grateful for this bit of humanity from this man, who had taught them all how unprepared they were for boot camp. Sammy wiped his mouth with his sleeve, no one was looking.

"You'll need to change that shirt too," said the sergeant.

Sammy spit out a "yes, sir" and made his way to the barracks. He wondered what they would be eating for supper. He was actually beginning to get hungry. He meandered into the barracks, took off his shirt, hit the shower quickly, and headed to mess. He had been given instructions to go to the back door of the mess hall to report for KP duty.

He was met at the back door of the kitchen by a lanky fellow who every one called Chef Phil. He was a Pilipino.

"Potatoes and beef tips" was what the menu said on the door of the kitchen when he finally arrived.

"Don't worry, kid," said the cook, "peeling potatoes is a skill that will actually do you some good out here."

"Thank you, sir" was what Sammy said as he arrived.

"You can eat first, no line here."

Mrs. Becker awoke to the sound of her daughter heaving in the toilet. She had morning sickness and was craving pickles dipped in barbeque sauce. The clock read seven a.m. sharp. She would get some coffee brewing soon.

As she walked around the corner, Bonnie was wiping her mouth with a rag from the sink. She then took a towel and dabbed the perspiration on her brow.

"You feel like a little breakfast?" asked Mrs. Becker.

"Actually, I'm feeling a little better. Coffee?"

For Sammy, there was no nausea, but there was perspiration. New to Sammy's vocabulary was 'Goddamit, motherfucker,' and a few other assorted colorful words of description. They were running, it was just after sun-up. They'd started the day at six a.m. looking straight ahead at attention, as the drill sergeant gave them the schedule of the day, drilling holes through them as he looked them directly in the eye.

Today, they would learn how to strip an M-16. They would later learn how to shoot an M-16, and then they would later in the week learn to duck and crawl while someone shot an M-16 above their heads.

"You don't have the hair to stand up in this drill!" was the advice given later, as they again got onto their knees.

The day ended with dinner across the shopping center with Chloe and Alicia, her youngest. They had just finished preparations to send out the wedding invitations. In about a week or two, they would send them out. Both Chloe and Bonnie's mother talked about the good ole days, when they had to learn life on the fly, as their husbands earned the bacon out in the field.

This is really living, thought Bonnie. She couldn't wait for tomorrow, she'd get to see Sammy.

The next evening found Sammy standing at attention again. This time in preparation for leave. Days turned into weeks, and Sammy was hardened like he had never been before. A passer-by might notice a calm confidence in the eyes that was beginning to develop. Bonnie would later tell him how she loved the man she saw him becoming. They spoke on the phone whenever they could. The sun was again setting. Soon, he would be going to see Bonnie. She'd be a sight for sore eyes.

Oils of Arizona
Mark Vaughn

They say that in the harbor called Pearl
Is a white mooring
Built above a sunken boat
Inside are those
Who never saw again
Light.

They spent their last minutes tapping
Tapping on walls that were muted
To sailors
In battle exhausted from the fight
In slick waters
That were polluted
They search the darkened water
'Till dawn's early light.

They felt their efforts were futile
Though great heroism was seen
And from it a nation awoke
From its stupor and dream.

Now the oils from the depths tell the tales
Down where Pearls can be made
For from the oils of the Arizona
Is a courage that has made many a sailor brave...

And in memory
Of those hidden in the depths
Flower petals fall
From maidens fair.

Remembering
Saying, "Lest we forget."

And from the oils
Starting in the depths
Comes the cry with mournful sigh
"Fare thee well."

Chapter Six
Pearl

It was about eighty degrees Fahrenheit with a steady breeze at the boat dock. The man with the captain's bars in the freshly pressed army uniform was standing by the small boat that would transport them out to the Arizona Memorial. Last night, Sammy had decompressed on a night boat cruise complete with meal and hula. You'd have hardly thought there was a gun being fired anywhere in the world.

Sammy approached, now in a uniform of his own. He was a marine now. The two saluted, then the captain proffered his hand. Sammy shook it.

"You did well, son," said Captain Becker. Sammy was a bit intimidated by the captain even when he wasn't in in his uniform, but now with a given oath and rank on his shoulders, he was even a bit more so. Captain John Becker did his best to ease the mild tension. Captain Becker was already a decorated war veteran. He had served in Vietnam, and had participated in the successful Inchon landings under MacArthur. He had been a non-com upon entering, but was recommended for OCS for his brief stint in Korea.

"Thank you, sir," said Sammy.

"I thought I'd get you away from Bonnie, and her mother.

Talk a little man to man."

They boarded the little schooner and were soon set adrift for the white mooring sitting above the sunken ship. Sammy was on leave and soon would be on his way to Vietnam. Captain Becker was on his way to the States from Vietnam.

"I figure you want to know what it's like to be in country, but I won't bore you with my brief encounters with the NVA. You're a good soldier and will know of it soon enough. About my daughter, son, she's never been happier, and you were a gentleman. You're a part of the family."

"Thank you, sir."

"And you don't have to call me sir when you can get away with it. You like sail fishing, Sammy?'

"Yes, sir, I mean, yes," said Sammy.

The captain chuckled. "Good. I have a charter lined up after this. We can get away with civilian clothes."

Sammy had always lived in fear of the captain. He was always sorry when he got Bonnie home past curfew, and usually stumbled over his words when answering questions. It had been a while since Captain Becker had seen Sammy. It was quite obvious to Captain Becker that Sammy had some newfound confidence and maturity. He had gotten to know Sammy's family, a good white family. It would help in the days ahead. Of course, Captain Becker was part of a new generation of Americans with a de-segregated military.

The boat docked on the mooring, and the two men stepped off.

"You ever been to Hawaii before, Sammy?" asked Captain Becker.

"No, sir, well, not that I remember. I was actually born in Hawaii. Mom and Dad were stationed here during the World

War. They have been back. I've seen the pictures," said Sammy.

"The town's changed a lot," said Captain Becker.

"Yes, sir," said Sammy. "That's what they say."

They walked quietly from there, through the entrance of the new constructed *USS Arizona* Memorial. The waters off the structure were emerald like the rest of the waters, except for the huge black shadow of a sunken battleship.

They walked past the remembrances to a place where the floor parted to reveal the waters underneath. There were roses and carnations floating on the surface. With a stiff salute, the two parted, then met in the alcove near the entrance.

It was quiet on the ride back. Finally, Captain Becker spoke.

"I still remember December 7, 1941. I was seventeen years old. I enlisted, along with a lot of other boys." His voice stifled a bit, catching.

"Yes, sir" was all Sammy said. "Dad was there. He told me he jumped under a bunk with a priest."

This made Captain Becker laugh. "Did he, now?" he said.

"I figure my dad knew some of those gentlemen. My mom told me about it. Dad always gets real quiet," said Sammy.

"Yeah, I know, I drink from time to time with your ole man."

"Yes, sir."

The boat rode on in silence. They departed, each their separate ways. Tomorrow, sail fishing. Monday, the big ride to Vietnam.

KENNEDY INCREASES AID TO SOUTH VIETNAMESE

In a public exchange of letters with South Vietnamese president Ngo Dinh Diem, President John F. Kennedy formally announces that the United States will increase aid to South Vietnam which would include the expansion of the U.S. troop commitment. Kennedy, concerned with the recent advances made by the communist insurgency movement in South Vietnam, wrote, "We shall promptly increase our assistance to your defense effort."

Kennedy's chief military adviser, Gen. Maxwell D. Taylor, and Special Assistant for National Security Affairs, Walt W. Rostow, had just returned from a fact-finding trip to Saigon and urged the president to increase U.S. economic and military advisory support to Diem. The military support was to include intensive training for local self-defense troops by American military advisers. Additionally, Taylor and Rostow advocated for a significant increase in airplanes, helicopters, and support personnel. In a secret appendix to their report, Taylor and Rostow recommended the deployment of 8,000 American combat troops, which could be used to support the South Vietnamese forces in combat operations against the insurgents. To overcome Diem's resistance to foreign troops—which he saw as a potential Viet Cong propaganda windfall—Taylor and Rostow suggested that the forces were to be called a 'flood control team.' Kennedy, who wanted to stop the communists but also wanted to be cautious about the degree of involvement, accepted most of the recommendations, but did not commit U.S. combat troops.

Chapter Seven
Letters

Dear Sammy,
I can't believe it's already the holiday season. I'm back in Chicago and missing you. I have mom, and Mrs. von Burger (other mom) to talk to, but our world has changed, and is still changing. I feel the baby growing inside me as it seems our lives are beginning to blossom as a family. I get word sometimes of Vietnam; of course, I am like all the other wives. Our code is not to speak about such things unless absolutely necessary. It's our duty so to speak. I have been to my own basic.

I am proud of you. You are more like Dad than you want to know, but your dad is a lot like my dad. He went a different way. And I am proud to be a wife of a Marine. I know you will make our family proud. I think I may move to the base. It would cut out the frequent commutes. We'd have our own place, and Sammy Jr. will need that. I want to name him Sammy.

I found out how you got your name. We are an eclectic bunch, aren't we? I feel I have lived years in a moment, and can't wait to see you home again.

Love forever,
Bonnie

Bonnie would often read through her past letters from Sammy in lonely moments. It had not even been a year of marriage. She hoped it would always be like this. Chloe said that it would be, but it would always be changing, like a pearl at the bottom of the ocean.

DEAR SAMMY (stop) I SAW BILLY (stop) TALK ABOUT A FAVORITE SON (stop) JUST A HIGH SCHOOL QUARTERBACK (stop) HE'S FLYING (stop) HE WORSHIPS YOU (stop) LETTER COMING ABOUT TO BUST AT SEAMS (STOP) LOVE BONNIE

Dear Bonnie,
I am in Vietnam. I guess you know. It's hot. The barracks are, in a word, hot. I'll try not to fret you with the day to day. I saw your dad one day in Saigon on leave. Saigon is an interesting town. In a word, It's not Chicago. The captain told me I could tell you this. We went camping together on the Ho Chi Minh trail, not far outside Saigon. It was peaceful, I'd bring Sammy Jr. to see it. He'd like the fireworks. But Chicago has much better fireworks, ask my dad.

I have discovered prayer again. The captain said I would. Dad said he has trouble with church now. Well, so do I, but I am certainly learning to pray again. Sometimes, at night, looking up at the stars, I feel a calm confidence. I know someone is looking out for us. More later.

Love always,
Sammy

Dear Sammy,

It's Thanksgiving. The holiday season is so festive. Only a few more months. I thought about our argument today. I was near the waterfront. Sammy Jr. kicked. I don't know why. I think he was saying I love you. And so am I. I hope you can get leave. But here or not, I have only begun to fight.

Love forever,
Bonnie

Chapter Eight
Jungle Tour

Sammy was taking point. This was not his first participation with the South Vietnamese. He was a forward adviser, low rank, and low rank had its privileges. He would never write Bonnie back home about this. He took chances out here; taking chances is what got him here in the first place. Sammy was just past eighteen, so he thought he might be nearly invincible. Stories at night on their encampment nearby with some of the regulars did nothing but fuel this fire. He had only been on point twice. He was good at being point. They said he was like a peacock.

    He was unsure of the name of the trail; he had a hard time with the Vietnamese sounds. He called it the Yellow Brick Road. The jungle was shaded but very steamy. On a good day, Sammy could put away a gallon of water. He had a kid on the way, but the kid was the furthest from his mind. This was like baseball, only better. He'd not really seen a good firefight yet. It was part of the reason they kept sending him out. The hair on the back of Sammy's neck began to stand up. He hit the deck.

    The first gunshot was drowned in the cacophony that followed. There was one other American with him. The rest were South Vietnamese.

Sammy's heart was reacting, and his head was in the dirt. Strange thoughts accompany such a moment, and his was, *So this is what Dad didn't tell me about.*

"Burger!" was all he heard. "Shitsville!"

Sammy could hardly move. He knew that they were in a mess, and backwards was the only real option other than keeping his head down. Whatever damn fool notion caused him to open fire, he didn't know.

There were gunshots, and Vietnamese voices. Sammy didn't understand a damn thing.

"Sammy, crawl your ass, Goddammit!" It was Sarge. He's the one who had gotten him into this mess. Of course, Sammy was happy to volunteer. There was more gunfire, and Sammy's body felt numb… but intact. He inched backward, facing forward. Then heard a loud noise to his right.

He raised his gun, it was Viet Cong. Still numb hands, trembling more now, Sammy crawled in earnest and felt a hand. They had formed up. The South Vietnamese made them proud that day. They stayed put. They saw some scurrying figures, then silence.

"You OK, Sammy?" was what Sammy heard as Sarge handed him his pack. "You lost this."

Sammy sucked in a deep breath. "Negative, sir" was all he said.

Sammy awoke to helicopter blades beating in the wind. Sarge was next to him, so was Captain Becker.

"You're gonna be all right, kid. You're gonna get to see Japan. You like Honolulu, don't you?"

"Yes, sir," said Sammy. He started crying.

Chapter Nine
Black Pearls – Japan

The first thing that Captain Becker noticed once he had left the base was that everything in it seemed too small for him. Everything seemed contained in small boxes, and a pagoda greeted him at the street corner. He was out for some fresh air. He would soon be going again to see his son-in law. Sammy had been flown to Japan after being stabilized. Captain Becker called home. It was a little more than a flesh wound and part of his colon had been removed. The abdomen entry missed the spinal cord but went out the back in dramatic fashion. Everything else worked fine, and Sammy being eighteen was perking up as if nothing had happened. He would groan loudly whenever he realized he'd been hit in the abdomen by a rather large caliber weapon.

They were going home together in a transport. It would soon be Christmas, and the captain would soon be a grand-pa. The ladies handled themselves as army wives should. Bonnie was still at home, but had considered moving to the base nearby. Later, he was told by 'Momma' that Bonnie had cried all night.

Captain Becker parked his car outside a rather small

building, and walked inside to make his purchase. What he bought was nothing more than some souvenirs. A shirt saying, "My dad went to Japan and all I got was this shirt" would have probably been enough. But he instead bought some extravagant dishware to be shipped later. On a captain's salary, it ate into his budget a little bit, but the Mrs. was good at managing their assets. She'd asked him about the dishes, and it was Christmas. And Sammy was coming home in something other than a box.

To think that just sixteen years ago, they had just concluded a war with Japan. The busy streets were in stark contrast to what could have been. He had been a MacArthur admirer. And since MacArthur's governorship, Japan seemed to be the better for it.

His other plans for when he got home was a 'de-briefing' with John. But that would be for after the kids went to bed. Decompression was good for the soul and the sanity, when done in proper amounts.

The ride back was non-eventful. The walk to Sammy's room was much the same.

"How you doing, son?" asked Captain Becker.

Sammy was sitting up in bed watching television.

"A-OK, sir" was what he said.

Dear Sammy,

I always hate to watch the news, but being a good girl with a good upbringing, I always do. It seems that more troops are on their way to Vietnam. At least, that's the rumors going through the rumor mill. Now I know you don't like President Kennedy as much as Dad, but I really like him. And it's not just because he looks good on TV. I like to hear him speak. I feel real comfortable with him in charge. I worry sometimes still, but I enjoy the ladies down at the base. I still live with Momma though. I am hoping you will be home soon. I'm really far along, shhhh—they will think we're bad. I'm real uncomfortable, sometimes afraid. But trying to be brave.

It sounds a bit silly sometimes, but I understand Mom more now and some of the things she'd say, and still says about Dad. I say them about you now.

You know about Dad's stories. When I see your mail clipped with sections missing, I know you are serving with Dad somewhere. Momma says his mail has mostly been that way. Mostly just names missing and places. Momma would tell me "he's a stubborn ass sometimes, but he's no fool," when I would worry about Daddy.

We're going to be parents soon. I miss you. Come home soon.

Love forever,
Bonnie

A week later, they were on board the grueling flight to Hawaii. Sammy handled the flight better than the captain.

While in Honolulu, Sammy stood in the harbor. The *USS Yorktown* was making anchor and next to it a new, modern *USS Enterprise*.

After a night in Hawaii, they were on a flight to Chicago.

Chapter Ten

Riding through the familiar streets of Chicago was a pleasant shock to the system. The Christmas lights lit up the Chicago night. A few turns and there was home, or what was now home; Bonnie was there. It was the Beckers' and it hadn't changed a bit. He'd head off to see Mom and Dad as soon as he got unpacked. The cab driver stopped the car and got out. Sammy got out of the back of the yellow cab. He heard Captain Becker shut the door on his side. The driver opened the trunk so they could get their bags. He carried Sammy's for him; Sammy was still hobbling from the battle wound. Together, they walked to the front porch of Captain Becker's home. New traditions and new places, but same ole Chicago.

    As they drew close to the porch, curtains were opened, the front door opened, and there was Bonnie and Mrs. Becker, with Jr in the wings. A few quick hugs and they were inside, with thoughts of sugar plumbs in their heads. A well ornamented Christmas tree was sitting by the window with several presents underneath. Christmas was about a week away.

    After polite small talk, Bonnie and Sammy headed for Mom and Dad's. The drive was the same length. But something was different about everything. The neighborhood seemed somehow smaller. They rounded the familiar corner through 15th and 58th, and there it was. Sammy caught his breath just a bit, but hardly anything noticeable, except to maybe Bonnie. But she didn't say anything, leaving the moment for him.

They pulled in the driveway. There was Pop. He had his coat on, covering his flannel shirt. But underneath it all was his famous white T-shirt. And mom was all smiles. Alicia ran out the door and gave him a big hug. Soon emerging from the doorway were his brothers, all looking a bit timid at this man who had left just a boy.

"I hear you made the play-offs," hollered Sammy to Billy.

"Yeah, we lost to Tillman Heights," said Billy.

"Made a good showing though," said Jon.

Sonny stood in the doorway. He had just started high school, skinny as a rail.

"Well, come on in," said Mom. Chloe von Burger was going to be a grandmother. She hugged her son Sammy. Sammy groaned slightly. "Oh, I forgot, you're a war hero now." She kissed his cheek.

"We've been looking after your sweetheart!" she said as she hugged Bonnie.

They walked in to Bing Crosby playing on the record player. The smell of Christmas in the air.

Only six more shopping days 'till Christmas, and Bonnie was due anytime.

Chapter Eleven
Christmas Blessings

"*O Come Let Us Adore Him, Christ the Lord.*" Sammy was actually singing. He had his beautiful wife next to him, Mom and Pop, and his brothers. The captain and Mrs. Becker had taken their leave this Christmas Eve, but would be up bright and early Christmas morning. They were members of a local AME church. Sammy would occasionally attend, but couldn't handle the preaching. He said it was worse than white churches. The captain would simply laugh at his disturbing remarks and sometimes mutter to the Mrs., "He's learning." Usually, Jon would not attend at all, but would go for an occasional confessional with the Catholic priest. But for this service, the whole family was there, and Chloe von Burger stood there proud as a peacock.

During the service, they lit candles and said some prayers. There were remarks on the Prince of Peace, and they closed with the song of the angels "Of Peace on Earth, Good Will to Men." During *Silent Night*, Jon von Burger had to leave. Chloe grabbed Sammy's arm. She shook her head.

At home, there was the traditional one present before Christmas, where everyone could choose one present from under the tree to open. Chloe von Burger had made Wessel.

And there were smiles all around when Alicia opened up her Barbie dress kit. Sonny got a guitar music book with some of the newer tunes in it. Billy got a fancy leather letterman's jacket. Bonnie got a new pair of shoes to add to her collection, which were already covering the closet floor. And Sammy got a small box with Dad's Distinguished Flying Cross.

"Dad?" was all he said.

"You've earned it, pass it on to Jr. when he gets old enough."

The next morning, the von Burgers and the Beckers got together for Christmas Dinner at the Beckers'. Barbara Becker was showing off her brand-new china from Japan.

"We thank thee for thy bountiful blessings, O Lord Our God. We thank thee for our safe return, and for the new addition who will soon be among us. Amen." said the captain, looking quite casual without his usual military outfit.

There was a smaller table for the youngsters who were quite happy to eat away from the adults. Jr. and Alicia were sitting together enjoying the Christmas glow. Except for the occasional "Momma, do I have to eat that?", they were quite content.

The talk at the table was mostly about family-related subjects. One was that Billy was doing quite well in his senior year and was thinking about the navy. Letters had been sent for a possible Annapolis appointment. There was no jealousy with the two brothers. Both were all smiles... Billy, a favorite as the second son. If there were awards to be won, it seemed that Billy would find a way to win them. He hardly got into trouble, and when he did, all were quick to excuse him and brush it under the rug. He took it all in stride.

Fathers sometimes might have a favorite, and you would think it would be Billy, because of how much trouble Sammy was. But Sammy got the Flying Cross as the first born. And both boys were very glad to see their older brother in one piece after being in the hospital in Japan.

"I applied to Jet Engine School," said Sammy.

All looked up. The implication quite clear.

"They said they didn't want me out in the field for a while," he said.

"Well done, son" is what he heard from Captain Becker as he met his dad's gaze.

Chapter Twelve
1962

Sammy was quiet, standing in the hall at Mom and Dad's. It was New Year's Eve and he had been run out of the hospital at eight p.m. Plenty of pictures had been taken, but he'd have to wait about a week for them. Sammy Jr. was almost a New Year's baby. Instead, he was a December 27 baby. He weighed in at eight pounds even. He was twenty inches long. Sammy and the grandmothers had gotten to hold him, Sammy for not very long. But mostly it was Bonnie who held him. Mom and baby were doing fine and would be coming home in a few days.

Sammy overheard his mother reading to Alicia, *The Legend of the Black Pearls* by Shawn Craft. Sammy peeked his head round the corner. His brothers were seeking other entertainment nearby at a New Year's Eve concert.

"You can come in if you want to," said Chloe.

"Sure," said Sammy.

"You can take some pointers, you might need to do this one day soon."

Sammy smiled, a bit uncomfortable in his own house, in what was once his own room. His room was temporarily at the Beckers'. But his roommate was at the hospital, so he was staying at Mom and Dad's tonight.

"Off in the land of the tropical sun, down near where the equator meets the sea, is a special bay. It was a harbor of tranquility for all who might happen upon it. It was said that the inlet was golden, but not because of gold deblumb, or any other treasure that might be there."

Chloe paused to show the pictures to Alicia. They were beautiful watercolors, with colors of the tropics.

"A volcano watched over the bay, and from it came the ingredients that would one day become beautiful stones. The dark, grainy dust that settled on the ocean floor and the gases from the deep that had blended into the ocean depths would seep into the large oysters that lived there."

Alicia had her fingers in her mouth. It was the middle two. "Vanilla and chocolate," she would say to anyone interested.

Chloe showed her the next pictures. "Alicia, honey, you need to stop that, or you might end up with braces," said Chloe.

Sammy smirked a little. He wondered if he had ever really been that little, but seemed to remember being told much the same thing during bedtime stories.

"The dark sand that would rest inside the oyster shell would cause great pain to its benefactor. And to quiet the pain, a beautiful crystalline coat would wrap around the unwelcomed guest. But the two together would work in a strange harmony to make the jewel that could be found enclosed inside."

A quick look at the next pictures, and again Alicia had her fingers in her mouth. Better than a pacifier, this time Mother did not protest.

"A lucky diver who might have traveled to this remote place could find the pearl inside, unique from others found in other bays. For its color was as ebony on a piano."

Alicia turned the page. "With it, one might find monetary blessing. But those that were wise would find treasures that could satisfy the soul. The pearls, even if not found, are said to bless the waters and bring serenity to the spirit of any who might in happenstance find them."

"Prayers, Momma?" asked Alicia. She folded her hands.

Alicia and her mother said together, "Now I lay me down to sleep, I pray the Lord my soul to keep… God Bless Momma and Daddy, and Billy and Sonny, and Jr. and baby Sammy.

"Don't forget Daddy, and Mr. and Mrs. Becker," said Chloe.

"And Bonnie too," said Alicia.

"Amen."

Sammy stood. "Goodnight, Mom," he said and headed for the sofa.

"Goodnight, son," said Chloe.

The New Year would have to come in without him. Sammy was bushed.

Chapter Thirteen
Jet Engine School

Sammy was sitting in a rocker, watching his little boy with his wife. He had a picture of them when they first arrived home. She was self-contemplative as she looked with appreciation and love at their new child. She nursed him as she rocked his rocker. In the room, there was a crib and a bed for the both of them. It was a small room; Bonnie's room once upon a time, converted into their family living quarters for the duration of Sammy's leave, which was just about over.

"There's Sammy Jr.," said a voice from around the corner. Two faces peered in and smiled from the door. "About ten more minutes, we'll need to get you going. Take your time. Bonnie, you coming with?"

"I think I'll say my good-byes here," said Bonnie. She was a bit melancholic, but was hiding it all behind a smile of motherly affection.

Sammy was beginning to understand the enormity of what he had gotten himself into. He had learned to feed, burp, and clothe Sammy Jr., but left the bathing up to Bonnie with a quiet assist in the background. At night, he would look at the little boy lost in his own thoughts. The couple slowly began to bond again when Sammy, after a sixty-day hospital leave, was now on his way once again. This time, posting himself to perhaps maintain contact with his brother Billy, who it appeared was destined to fly.

Billy was in boot camp. With an early graduation and leave from school, he was planning to walk in the spring with the end of the school year. He had applied for Annapolis, but even with their dad's service record and glowing recommendations, it was a long shot.

The television was going around the corner. Alicia, Chloe's youngest, was playing on the floor. Chloe and Barbara Becker were talking in hushed tones. The captain sat in his recliner; Sammy stood by the door for a bit and watched both rooms, nervously fidgeting with a pencil.

On the television was a picture of John Glenn boarding *Friendship 7*. Alicia would pause from her play to look up from time to time. "Look, Momma, the space man." It was a long time till *Sesame Street*, if ever today.

Sammy walked back into the room. "May I hold him before I go?'

"You don't have to ask permission, but I do like that in a man," said Bonnie. She stood, still a little sore but coming along just fine. Sammy Sr. awkwardly held Jr. in his arms. Then carefully handed him back. He kissed Bonnie on the cheek, and then headed for the door.

"It won't be long," he said quickly, and grabbed his bag. He was much stronger, healing very well. But he would have spent his last days on the Ho Chi Minh trail if he could help it. Right now, he was likely to be a career man. Likely, but everyone knew Sammy.

"Ready to go, son?" asked the captain; he'd be shoving off soon himself. He had requested this leave to tend to his family. It would be a long while before he came back again. Sammy was in a man's world now, and he would be looking after himself on this next tour. They'd probably see each other in the demilitarized zone.

Chloe, Alicia, Mr. and Mrs. Becker, and Jr. along with Sammy, all packed into the family station wagon. Sammy threw his bags in the back. The captain's was already there.

The drive to the bus station was longer, and shorter than the one on which they arrived. Soon, Sammy was situated; he hugged his mother and Mrs. Becker. Alicia hugged his leg tenderly. Sammy saluted the captain, who saluted him back. Dad had said his goodbyes last night. Sammy asked permission to place his medal in a memorable location. His dad said yes. Then muttered, "What better place." They hugged rather than saluted. Mr. von Burger was somewhere in Chicago, doing his duty as a cop.

"Good hunting, soldier" is what he heard as he left. He didn't look back till he boarded the bus. Only then to a familiar car pulling away from the bus station. He had a tough school ahead. If he qualified high enough, he might even work on Billy's plane.

In the evening, Sammy saw in the news that *Friendship 7* had successfully landed. The bus route south would take him down a road he had seen in the news only a little over a year ago. It would run through Tupelo, Mississippi. As the bus moved south then west, slowly making the journey west to its final destination, the nation seemed at peace. Sammy often would sit with a newspaper, now paying too much more than the sports section. In Southeast Asia, trouble still brewed. The

Cuban Missile Crisis had come and gone. America was in the midst of a Space Race shadowing a bitter Cold War that threatened at any time to ignite the world again, as it had been in his father's younger days as a flyer. And now for the first time really since he had married, he felt the burden of being the head of his household.

He flipped through the remainder of the paper, comics, and weather, then sports. He saw in the sports section that spring training was underway. Maybe he might catch a game in Arizona.

His last thoughts, as the bus pulled into the station where he would debark, were of his family.

INTERLUDE

John Fitzgerald Kennedy,
Ich bin ein Berliner Speech, June 26, 1963

I am proud to come to this city as the guest of your distinguished mayor, who has symbolized throughout the world the fighting spirit of West Berlin. And I am proud to visit the Federal Republic with your distinguished chancellor, who for so many years has committed Germany to democracy and freedom and progress, and to come here in the company of my fellow American, General Clay, who has been in this city during its great moments of crisis, and will come again if ever needed.

Two thousand years ago, the proudest boast was *"civis Romanus sum."* Today, in the world of freedom, the proudest boast is *"Ich bin ein Berliner."*

I appreciate my interpreter translating my German!

There are many people in the world who really don't understand, or say they don't, what is the great issue between the free world and the communist world. Let them come to Berlin. There are some who say that communism is the wave of the future. Let them come to Berlin. And there are some who say in Europe and elsewhere, we can work with the communists. Let them come to Berlin. And there are even a few who say that it is true that communism is an evil system, but it permits us to make economic progress. *Lass' sie nach Berlin kommen.* Let them come to Berlin.

Freedom has many difficulties and democracy is not perfect, but we have never had to put a wall up to keep our people in, to prevent them from leaving us. I want to say, on behalf of my countrymen, who live many miles away on the other side of the Atlantic, who are far distant from you, that they take the greatest pride that they have been able to share with you, even from a distance, the story of the last eighteen years. I know of no town, no city, that has been besieged for eighteen years that still lives with the vitality and the force, and the hope and the determination of the city of West Berlin. While the wall is the most obvious and vivid demonstration of the failures of the communist system, for all the world to see, we take no satisfaction in it, for it is, as your mayor has said, an offense not only against history but an offense against humanity, separating families, dividing husbands and wives and brothers and sisters, and dividing a people who wish to be joined together.

What is true of this city is true of Germany—real, lasting peace in Europe can never be assured as long as one German out of four is denied the elementary right of free men, and that is to make a free choice. In eighteen years of peace and good faith, this generation of Germans has earned the right to be free, including the right to unite their families and their nation in lasting peace, with good will to all people. You live in a defended island of freedom, but your life is part of the main. So, let me ask you as I close, to lift your eyes beyond the dangers of today, to the hopes of tomorrow, beyond the freedom merely of this city of Berlin, or your country of Germany, to the advance of freedom everywhere, beyond the wall to the day of peace with justice, beyond yourselves and ourselves to all mankind.

Freedom is indivisible, and when one man is enslaved, all are not free. When all are free, then we can look forward to that day when this city will be joined as one, and this country and this great continent of Europe, in a peaceful and hopeful globe. When that day finally comes, as it will, the people of West Berlin can take sober satisfaction in the fact that they were in the front lines for almost two decades.

All free men, wherever they may live, are citizens of Berlin, and, therefore, as a free man, I take pride in the words *"Ich bin ein Berliner."*

Chapter Fourteen
Pearl Farmers

Proverbs 2:1,2,4

My son, if thou wilt receive my words and hide my commandments with thee so that thou inclines my ear toward wisdom... If thou seekest her as silver and search for her as hid treasure.

Lady Wisdom

...In colors of yellow
As fading leaves
Some with grays
Some ivory
Some colder than black lava flows
Where the heat is intense
And great pressure is known
There in the quiets
Far from the sun
Is where Lady Wisdom
A timeless beauty is won.

"Sounds self-serving," said Jon. A hand mitt for the stove suddenly startled him as it hit him in the head.

"Ouch," said Jon with a smile. "I meant, it was good."

Alicia could be heard playing in her room down the hall. She was talking to her stuffed animals. She set them up in rows and taught them lessons as their schoolteacher. She ignored Mom and Dad when she did.

"There's a letter from Sammy on the coffee table," said Chloe. "He sounds homesick already. He's glad to be stateside though. He's thinking of maybe moving Bonnie and Sammy Jr. out there with him."

Jon picked up the letter and skimmed it.

"Jet engines. Does he know Billy is taking flying lessons?" asked Jon.

"He knows," said Chloe.

"I guess we should move," said Jon.

He got the other mitten in the head.

Jon read the letter as Alicia ran into the kitchen chasing her mother.

Dear Mom and Dad,

Another day, another dollar. Jet engines in the morning, jet engines in the evening, jet engines when the sun goes down. There's nothing like isolation on an army base. An Air Corp Army base. They're not teaching us to be grease monkeys, but miracle workers.

There's not much to do but practice and study. I may get some leave, but probably will be shipped out on graduation. It's not too far now, I am counting the days. Got a week under my belt.

I've thought about moving Bonnie, but I'd rather move her to some place like Pearl. She says Chicago is just fine with her and Junior. I guess that means no.

Not too much news. I could bore you with the bus ride and the class work. You taught me a lot of this stuff working on cars, but it's a little more complicated. Turbo engines are a lot louder, I am told.

I heard a Russian woman flew into space. Maybe you should tell Bonnie. We could get together maybe, turbo engines and rockets.

I enjoyed being home. I enjoyed it a little too much. You told me it might get like this one day. I guess I'm growing up—twenty-one, I can legally drink everywhere now. Good thing the military knows that.

Jon laughed and thought, *So does the city of Chicago.*

Jon skimmed through the remainder of the letter to

Love,

Twenty-one with a purple heart. I guess Mom always tells me "a chip off the ole' block."

Chapter Fifteen
A Second Graduation

It was a different gymnasium. It was a different crowd of people. But it was the same von Burgers. Chloe was again as proud as a peacock, sitting on the edge of her seat as her second born received his diploma to a standing ovation. Billy said the attention he got for his athletics embarrassed him.

As he walked across the stage, Chloe could see him blush, heard Jon chuckle just slightly, hardly audible, taking it all in. And out of the corner of her eye, she saw Bonnie grabbing hold of a rambunctious Sammy Jr. Alicia was next to her and spellbound. Sonny was next to her clapping politely. He was the shiest of the three boys. He was learning the guitar.

In that instant moment in time, like a 360-degree Polaroid, Billy waved to the crowd, and then took his seat.

It took a while to finally reach him after the graduation. There was another familiar face standing nearby. He simply smiled subtly to Chloe, and left her with Jon. Only she knew that this favorite son was that stranger's son. Jon probably knew, he knew of him.

It was the only thing that clouded a nearly perfect day. There were some stares at Bonnie and Sammy Jr., but they were mere distractions. For the most part, everyone's attention was on Billy. And when he took Sammy Jr. into his arms, the crowd cooed. Bonnie smiled.

Everyone loved this young man.

"Congratulations, son," said a man in a uniform. He was the one that had helped him get his flying lessons. The hopes were a fast track through flight school. Jon shook his hand, said a few words, and the two walked off together for a few minutes, then Jon returned.

Chloe lowered her head slightly, a brief look of worry passed over her face. Then she smiled again as Jon returned to her side.

Quickly, jokes lightened the mood.

They were in their station wagon after the crowd had dispersed. For some reason, she was a bit embarrassed by its appearance now. Bonnie noticed. She patted Chloe's shoulder. Chloe briefly held Bonnie's hand.

"The Hamburger House!" she heard Alicia holler. Then a horn at a worse-looking clunker drove up next to them. It was Billy's car.

"The Hamburger House?" he asked.

"Hamburger House it is," said Jon.

Two clunkers followed each other out into traffic and turned on to the highway to the Hamburger House.

The band on the stage was dressed in what looked like a cross between zoot suits and something one might wear to church. There was a small drum set on the stage, with everyone else in the band holding a guitar of some kind, and tending to a microphone. Sonny was playing the drums. The tunes they were playing were hits of the time.

The occasion? Sammy was home.

Chapter Sixteen
Bus Rides

The bus ride was south. Bonnie was not happy about it. She continually went on about how hard it was going to be to get anything done, and how hard it would be for a negro woman to even live on a base in Texas. Sammy promised her letters and a visit when he could. Bonnie looked at her father. Sammy got his bags and headed out the door. Sammy Jr. poked his head around the corner.

"It will be all right for her here until we get things settled," said the captain.

"Come here, kid," said Sammy. Sammy Jr. ran around the corner and gave his father a quick hug. He had asked the uncomfortable question about his skin tone. Sammy said, "It's the heart that counts." That seemed to settle it for Sammy Jr.

Now he was upset that this man who was his daddy was about to leave again. Sammy was in between schools. He had tried to talk Bonnie into moving to the base during his training.

That's what led to the argument. The house seemed to grow smaller as his family grew larger. He couldn't even remember who brought up the idea of buying a house. Captain Becker had chuckled. That didn't help.

The reality of the situation was that he had to get through

this school to pay the bills, and it was a tough school. What awaited him after that was probably another tour of duty in Vietnam. This time as a jet mechanic.

Sammy stood to go, shook Captain Becker's hand, and gave a half salute to Mrs. Becker. He was not use to calling her Betty yet.

"Sammy?" said Bonnie in a heartfelt way. He looked up. "I love you."

Sammy smiled. "I love you too."

He hopped in the cab and was on his way to the bus station. It would take nearly a day to get there by the bus route. Plenty of time for thinking.

Down the road at the von Burgers' was a very similar scene.

Jon von Burger was waiting at the car for Billy. Sonny was standing on the porch as Billy said goodbye to Alicia, his little sister, and then to his current flame Rhonda. Rhonda was dressed in a short skirt with her hair fixed in a bun. She was the epitome of your All-American girl, a perfect complement to the All-American boy.

Billy was off to basic. It was a southern destination as well. It was in sunny Florida. There was not the same commitment to his girl. They were not married, but he wanted to hold on to her. Billy was not known for his long dating relationships with women.

He kissed her and hopped into the family Chevrolet. He waved to Sonny, who would hold down the fort with Mom, and Dad took him to the bus station. Sammy had already boarded his. With the shrill squeak of a loose fan belt, the car backed out of the drive-way.

Rhonda went and stood with Alicia, then said her goodbyes to Sonny and Mrs. von Burger.

Billy headed down the road in silence. He wondered

quietly what basic would be like. He wondered what life would now be like. For the first time in a long time, maybe in his life, Billy was a little unsettled about his future.

*Martin Luther King's 'I Have a Dream' speech,
August 28, 1963*

I am happy to join with you today in what will go down in history as the greatest demonstration for freedom in the history of our nation.

Five score years ago, a great American, in whose symbolic shadow we stand today, signed the Emancipation Proclamation. This momentous decree came as a great beacon light of hope to millions of Negro slaves who had been seared in the flames of withering injustice. It came as a joyous daybreak to end the long night of their captivity.

But one hundred years later, the Negro still is not free. One hundred years later, the life of the Negro is still sadly crippled by the manacles of segregation and the chains of discrimination. One hundred years later, the Negro lives on a lonely island of poverty in the midst of a vast ocean of material prosperity. One hundred years later, the Negro is still languished in the corners of American society and finds himself in exile in his own land. And so we have come here today to dramatize a shameful condition. In a sense, we've come to our nation's capital to cash a check.

When the architects of our republic wrote the magnificent words of the Constitution and the Declaration of Independence, they were signing a promissory note to which every American was to fall heir. This note was a promise that all men—yes, black men as well as white men—would be guaranteed the unalienable rights of life, liberty, and the pursuit of happiness.

It is obvious today that America has defaulted on this promissory note insofar as her citizens of color are concerned. Instead of honoring this sacred obligation, America has given the Negro people a bad check; a check which has come back marked 'insufficient funds.'

But we refuse to believe that the bank of justice is bankrupt. We refuse to believe that there are insufficient funds in the great vaults of opportunity of this nation. And so we have come to cash this check, a check that will give us upon demand the riches of freedom and the security of justice.

We have also come to this hallowed spot to remind America of the fierce urgency of now. This is no time to engage in the luxury of cooling off or to take the tranquilizing drug of gradualism.

Now is the time to make real the promises of democracy. Now is the time to rise from the dark and desolate valley of segregation to the sunlit path of racial justice. Now is the time to lift our nation from the quick sands of racial injustice to the solid rock of brotherhood. Now is the time to make justice a reality for all of God's children.

It would be fatal for the nation to overlook the urgency of the moment. This sweltering summer of the Negro's legitimate discontent will not pass until there is an invigorating autumn of freedom and equality. 1963 is not an end, but a beginning. Those who hope that the Negro needed to blow off steam and will now be content will have a rude awakening if the nation returns to business as usual.

There will be neither rest nor tranquility in America until the Negro is granted his citizenship rights. The whirlwinds of revolt will continue to shake the foundations of our nation until the bright day of justice emerges.

But there is something that I must say to my people who stand on the warm threshold which leads into the palace of justice. In the process of gaining our rightful place, we must not be guilty of wrongful deeds. Let us not seek to satisfy our thirst for freedom by drinking from the cup of bitterness and hatred.

We must forever conduct our struggle on the high plane of dignity and discipline. We must not allow our creative protest to degenerate into physical violence. Again and again, we must rise to the majestic heights of meeting physical force with soul force. The marvelous new militancy which has engulfed the Negro community must not lead us to a distrust of all white people, for many of our white brothers, as evidenced by their presence here today, have come to realize that their destiny is tied up with our destiny. And they have come to realize that their freedom is inextricably bound to our freedom. We cannot walk alone. And as we walk, we must make the pledge that we shall march ahead. We cannot turn back.

There are those who are asking the devotees of civil rights, "When will you be satisfied?" We can never be satisfied as long as the Negro is the victim of the unspeakable horrors of police brutality. We can never be satisfied as long as our bodies, heavy with the fatigue of travel, cannot gain lodging in the motels of the highways and the hotels of the cities.

We cannot be satisfied as long as the Negro's basic mobility is from a smaller ghetto to a larger one. We can never be satisfied as long as our children are stripped of their selfhood, and robbed of their dignity, by signs stating "for whites only."

We cannot be satisfied as long as a Negro in Mississippi

cannot vote and a Negro in New York believes he has nothing for which to vote.

No, no, we are not satisfied, and we will not be satisfied until justice rolls down like waters and righteousness like a mighty stream.

I am not unmindful that some of you have come here out of great trials and tribulations. Some of you have come fresh from narrow jail cells. Some of you have come from areas where your quest for freedom left you battered by the storms of persecution and staggered by the winds of police brutality. You have been the veterans of creative suffering. Continue to work with the faith that unearned suffering is redemptive.

Go back to Mississippi, go back to Alabama, go back to South Carolina, go back to Georgia, go back to Louisiana, go back to the slums and ghettos of our northern cities, knowing that somehow this situation can and will be changed. Let us not wallow in the valley of despair, I say to you today, my friends.

So even though we face the difficulties of today and tomorrow, I still have a dream. It is a dream deeply rooted in the American dream.

I have a dream that one day this nation will rise up and live out the true meaning of its creed: "We hold these truths to be self-evident; that all men are created equal."

I have a dream that one day on the red hills of Georgia, the sons of former slaves and the sons of former slave owners will be able to sit down together at the table of brotherhood.

I have a dream that one day even the state of Mississippi, a state sweltering with the heat of injustice, sweltering with the heat of oppression, will be transformed into an oasis of freedom and justice.

I have a dream that my four little children will one day live in a nation where they will not be judged by the color of their skin but by the content of their character. I have a dream today.

I have a dream that one day down in Alabama with its vicious racists, with its governor having his lips dripping with the words of interposition and nullification, one day right down in Alabama little black boys and black girls will be able to join hands with little white boys and white girls as sisters and brothers. I have a dream today.

I have a dream that one day every valley shall be exalted, every hill and mountain shall be made low, the rough places will be made plain, and the crooked places will be made straight, and the glory of the Lord shall be revealed, and all flesh shall see it together.

This is our hope. This is the faith that I will go back to the South with. With this faith, we will be able to hew out of the mountain of despair a stone of hope. With this faith we will be able to transform the jangling discords of our nation into a beautiful symphony of brotherhood. With this faith we will be able to work together, to pray together, to struggle together, to go to jail together, to stand up for freedom together, knowing that we will be free one day.

This will be the day when all of God's children will be able to sing with new meaning, "My country 'tis of thee, sweet land of liberty, of thee I sing. Land where my fathers died, land of the Pilgrims' pride, from every mountainside, let freedom ring."

And if America is to be a great nation, this must become true. And so let freedom ring from the prodigious hilltops of New Hampshire. Let freedom ring from the mighty mountains of New York. Let freedom ring from the heightening Alleghenies of Pennsylvania. Let freedom ring from the snow-capped Rockies of Colorado. Let freedom ring from the curvaceous slopes of California. But not only that; let freedom ring from the Stone Mountain of Georgia. Let freedom ring from Lookout Mountain of Tennessee. Let freedom ring from every hill and molehill of Mississippi. From every mountainside, let freedom ring.

And when this happens, and when we allow freedom ring, when we let it ring from every village and every hamlet, from every state and every city, we will be able to speed up that day when all of God's children, black men and white men, Jews and gentiles, Protestants and Catholics, will be able to join hands and sing in the words of the old Negro spiritual, "Free at last! Free at last! Thank God Almighty, we are free at last!"

Chapter Seventeen
SHOT!

It was the same exact restaurant they had eaten at the night before. How could it be? Bobby and Sammy were recollecting old times. Last night, their wives had been there. Tonight, well, tonight was two friends getting ready to head out. There was no duty station today other than to watch. President Kennedy had been shot. But duty called. For Sammy, he was stunned. This man he didn't completely like, mostly because of his father-in-law's influence, had made an impression on his life. He would vote democrat in the next election.

Bobby felt like Billy was the smarter of the bunch. And he had liked President Kennedy from the start.

The electricity of the favorite eating place was gone. It was as if someone had taken the oxygen out of the room. All seemed a bit sullen, going about routine to pass the day. No one expected this.

"Remember what you said," said Sammy over his beer.

"I know," said Bobby.

He took a deep swallow of his. "Well."

"I'll be ready for you. I got in too. How many places could they station us?"

Bobby looked up with a slight grimace.

There was almost a laugh in the silence. Then both remembered. The president had been shot.

They ate the rest of their dinner quietly while watching the black and white in the corner of the room.

They paid their tab.

Duty…

Chapter Eighteen
Goldwater

Sammy was on leave. He had become well known for his hard work and loyalty. The word around jet school was that the only thing that seemed to slow him down was his mouth and temper. He didn't drink much, and only for show. Most of it was his upbringing and his family. He came home with a black eye one night and couldn't remember how he got it. He had become a staunch Democrat. You couldn't call him a yellow dog because he didn't like being called a dog. The assassination of Kennedy shook him as it did the whole nation. He found a comfort in his leadership. He liked Lyndon Johnson. His people were like the rainbow, and this man liked the colors made by a prism.

He was on leave, on the phone, trying to be a good husband. His beautiful wife was often too far away, and when he was home, he was often too far away.

"Did you hear the speech?" asked Bonnie. "I asked Daddy about it."

"You mean Ronald Reagan's speech?" asked Sammy.

"Yeah, it made me wish he were a presidential candidate. Didn't help out Harry Truman," said Bonnie. "He was a little bit like Kennedy."

"Yeah," said Sammy. "I'm not going to vote for Goldwater."

"Well, if it's any comfort to you, Daddy's not going to vote for Goldwater either, but he liked Ronald Reagan. He said he reminded him of Kennedy a little."

"Kennedy? I suppose," Sammy said. "So, other than politics, what else has been going on?"

"Sammy Jr. has taken to chasing lizards," said Bonnie.

"Did he catch any?"

"No, came home with a tail and wanted to save it in a jar," said Bonnie.

Sammy laughed. "Maybe a little formaldehyde."

"Sammy Jr. wanted to give it back, so we sat it on the front porch. He said he was sure Santa Clause might be able to help."

There was a quiet pause, Sammy was horrible with words. "Bonnie—"

"I know, honey, I know."

That was good enough for him. He hated misting. When he did, he rushed to find an exit and a place to hide.

"Gotta go," he said.

"I love you," said Bonnie.

"I love you too."

He had leave soon. He missed home. But home was never home anymore.

Chapter Nineteen
The Race

It was one of those rare times when the two brothers would meet. There was a social gathering involving racing cars supped up by jet engines. The military usually frowned on such events, but it was good for morale. They had a few fairly successful events, and quite often the event was open to the public.

The cars involved were a 1960 Ford Falcon Convertible, with an ejection seat, and a 1942 Chevrolet Fleetline Starlight of the front. They said it was used to transport important military personal in Great Britain during World War II. Everyone doubted this, and everyone's money was on the newer sports car. There was no ejection seat in the older car, which the drivers said was actually a blessing. They each had a jet engine strapped to the back. The Starlight had a McDonnell engine used in F4 aircraft. The Ford Falcon had a Convair engine of nondescript origin. It was pieced together, but sound. It had been through a test run several times already.

Billy was seated in the stands. The pilots were not allowed to be in the driver's seats. Only jet engine mechanics with some drag racing experience. At that particular event, nearly all the jet engine mechanics had drag racing experience.

Sammy was not driving, but he was on the pit crew of the Falcon. No one really wanted to take credit for the other engine unless it won.

Sammy spoke with the driver of the Falcon as he put on his crash helmet, gave him a thumbs up, and got out of the way. They were near Edwards. They had bussed some people in for this event, even having press coverage. Cheers erupted from the stands as a gun went off and the two cars raced across the desert. There was dust, then flame, some commented on the g's the drivers might be pulling. The Convair won. Sammy threw his hat down in honest disgust. He had placed a bet on his car. He would not say how much he lost.

Chapter Twenty
August 30, 1967

The hum of the plane engine dominated any other sound, including any effort at conversation. Sammy and Billy were strapped to a seat in a C-140 transport en route to Da Nang. There were occasional bumps as the air mixed. The convection currents moved them along. The hint of a shoreline was ahead of them, outside the windows, but those inside wouldn't see much. They would simply wait until the plane came in for a landing. It had been a long flight from Pearl. Billy looked around the plane at its occupants as Sammy snoozed. On Sammy's lap was a half-finished copy of H.G. Wells' *The War of the Worlds*. Both were fans of the famous radio broadcast, which was benign science fiction, and they also enjoyed other world adventure books such as Jules Verne. Both were avid readers and faithful television watchers.

The newspaper headlines spoke of some of the new advances in science. A man in South Africa was making plans for a heart wing. They even spoke of a heart transplant. The headline of the *Chicago Tribune* read that Thurgood Marshall had been nominated by the Senate to be the first black man to serve as an associate Justice of the Supreme Court. It also made a note, in the corner of the front page, that The Viet Cong struck a jail in Quang Ngai. He and Sammy were part of a move by the president to send more troops to Vietnam. 45,000 it was on the next page. They were mere fighting men lost in the shuffle. But Billy was itching for a fight.

Billy had been in F-100s out of Flight Training. It had not been long since Annapolis. He had been the most available bachelor in Chicago while he was home, but now the least available. He had moved into F-4 Phantoms. He had chosen a Marine route to completion. So, Da Nang would be home for him for a while.

Sammy had pressed for jet engine school. With a second tour in between, he was an old timer now in his unit, but new to jets. They had the luck to land a similar duty, something rarely done, but given a turned head to because of the privilege of knowing those with rank and clout. It was a quiet authority that never was heard but always felt.

It had been a quick four years for Billy, call sign 'Billy Boy.' It had been followed by flight training and jet training. He had been promoted to F-4s though the F-100 pilots were nothing to be trifled with. The hellcats were ominous in battle, as aggressive as they were antiquated. But you shouldn't tell a hellcat pilot that. Tactically, they were as important as any supersonic support, or attack plane. Extremely versatile. The attraction of jets was obvious, and his strange desire of the prop planes was not. Maybe deep inside all of them, there was a hellcat waiting to get out. His dad had ended up in Corsairs. There were still a few of those around.

One thing he knew was that while his dad was still fond of it, Billy hated the name Billy Boy. How his classmates had discovered this was still a mystery to him. Sammy snored next to him as the plane began to descend. Da Nang was out far enough to feel fairly confident in landing. But no landing was a routine one in Vietnam. He looked again around the plane. All of them were air support, pilots, and maintenance.

The plane made its pattern turn and cut the engines. The increased convection woke Sammy. His book slid off onto the floor.

Sammy sat up as the plane began its turn onto final. The comforting jolt of the landing with the air brake let them know they were in Da Nang.

It was a heluva time to be in Vietnam. Thank God, he was in Jets.

Chapter Twenty-One
Emptying Nest

Jon sat outside on the porch. He could hear Sonny in the garage, playing away on his guitar. Jon had finally given in to the noise, and now actually kind of enjoyed it. Sonny was getting better. His long hair, which was pulled back in a ponytail, still irritated the fool out of Jon, but it was nice to have a son at home. His visit with Billy before being stationed was far too short. And while he saw Junior, Sammy's son, fairly regularly, he saw Sammy less and less. He was every bit a family man, and a soldier.

Alicia, now a budding adolescent, and Sonny were all that were left. Sonny had asked his dad if he wanted him to go into the military, and they had decided that they would let fate take its course. He would register for the draft in two months.

Jon dreaded the day. He knew Uncle Sam would require service of his third son. He wasn't against their service. But he was against the deep gnawing in his gut with each news account, and each deployment. Being a veteran, he knew too much sometimes.

Sammy was serving well, but his recuperation from the flesh wound in country still weighed on.

2nd Lt. William von Burger – Personal Journal

As I continue my personal journal of war experience, I realize that things of a childish nature have become important to me. With my barrack in Da Nang, at times when I close my eyes, I realize that the child's prayer taught to me by my mother gives me comfort.

"Now I lay me down to sleep, I pray the Lord my Soul to keep. If I should die before I wake, I pray the Lord my soul to take."

When I close my eyes, there is no longer any control. I might wake to trouble, or be headed into trouble. On a peaceful day, the warmth of the sun heartens my soul and gives me inner strength. Another night has come and gone, and I have lived to face another day.

I have always wanted to write. I have a book idea that I might run by my little sister, Alicia. She loves stories, and writes some in a childish way herself. I have read many a book to her at bedtime for my mother in her place. Maybe I can take this concept and develop it into something that will outlast me.

The question for me is: do I really want my name on it? Maybe a pen name.

Hmmmmm… something to think of. I hope no one reads this journal, I sure would never want to publish this.

Lt. Billy von Burger, call sign Billy Boy

Chapter Twenty-Two
The Tarmac

The tarmac and the hangar were much different from the bunker and the barracks. It was certainly different from being in-country. It was Da Nang. Technically, it was in-country. The jets and jet engines he serviced were certainly making an impact in-country. Sammy felt at home. This place had a strange feel of being more home right now than home. It bothered him some, but only when he dwelt on it.

What he dwelt on mostly here was the occasional mischief that might suddenly arise, and the jet that failed to return home. They were servicing F-100s mostly. Their mission was support of the bombers. They were aerial reconnaissance otherwise known as CAP support.

Sammy had been to Da Nang before. It was on his last tour. He didn't remember much about his departure. He was unconscious on his way to Japan after sustaining a wound to the abdomen in combat. He rubbed his belly. As good as new. He did it sub-consciously now, always grateful he was still in one piece. The temperature was a balmy ninety-five degrees or higher on most days. Winter-time was a drop below ninety-five. Today was not much different from most days. Sammy's day was spent with his face in an engine and a wrench in his hand. Today, however, at the end of his shift, he would be meeting Billy. He was flying in. He had just been assigned duty, and would be stationed in Da Nang.

Having a Purple Heart and a tour of duty under his belt had its advantages. He knew Billy had dreams of jet fighters, so he thought he might try to move in that direction. There was an opening for Jet Engine School and he put his name in for it. This was much better duty than the Ho Chi Minh trail.

Billy was going to join up with the John F Kennedy station, out in the Gulf of Tonkin. The F-100 sabres were famous for their use in Korea. Billy was mostly F-4. His mission was not much different than Sammy's air group, but he would be flying the aircraft. Sammy felt his sanity was more intact being on the ground. Billy disputed this.

They were to meet at the air base, and then to eat locally. After they said their hellos, they would likely begin this debate again. Billy always had an eye for the women, so Sammy was curious how he would do in Da Nang. Good thing they were flying off-shore. Their mother had asked Sammy to make sure Billy stayed out of trouble. Sammy was married, after all.

It was nearing the end of Sammy's shift. He was ready to pack up shop and head in.

"Good hunting," he heard as he wandered toward the barracks. He turned to see.

Chapter Twenty-Three
SHOT – April 5, 1968

"I'm in Da Nang, I don't have long. They let me call," said Sammy when he got Bonnie on the line. "What I want to know is, are you in any danger?"

"Honey, I'm with your momma and my momma," said Bonnie.

"Good," said Sammy in a quiet tone.

"Junior's just fine. Your dad is working a lot," said Bonnie.

"Good ole' Dad," said Sammy. He wondered how much more.

"Junior's reading now," she said.

"Oh good," said Sammy, a million miles away.

"Rough duty, I know."

"I just am glad to hear your voice. I miss you," said Sammy.

"We miss you too, love," she said.

Sammy smiled. It was the first smile in a while. He finished his tour, it was a horribly messy tour. "I don't really get away with it."

"Bobby's here," said Sammy.

"Oh, OK."

"Love you, better go," said Sammy.

They all knew Bobby kept his head on straight and could be the eyes for Sammy's blind ones.

Martin Luther King Jr. was dead. He had read his speech again. It was reprinted in the news. He wished he had appreciated the man more.

Chapter Twenty-Four
July 1968 – Mexico Olympics

Sammy promised Dad he'd try to catch some of the Olympics. He told them that one day they might have an Olympic moment like his. He was sitting with some of his mechanic mates with a black and white TV. The picture was absolutely horrible.

"These blokes won first and second in the 800-meter," said the first lieutenant. He was of Irish decent. "I always love the awards ceremony. At their best, they show harmony."

"Put on a wig," said a voice from the crowd. All looked, no one knew him, but he had major leaves on him. He quickly exited the scene much to the relief of all present.

Then Sammy heard, "What are they doing?"

Sammy looked up. Two black athletes on the awards stands were raising their fists in silent protest during the national anthem. Sammy's mouth stood agape, and he looked bum-fuzzled. He was a bit stunned by the whole thing.

"Bastards," he heard some say close by, it was the lieutenant. "So much for world harmony."

Sammy felt a few piercing glances come his way, then look down. He had nothing to say. But he watched the whole thing. He wondered what the captain would say. He wondered if Bonnie would see. He wondered about that little tyke he bounced on his knee.

"They shot Martin Luther King Jr." is all he said very quietly without much justification. He stood to leave, the magic of the Olympics ebbing away. He walked so freely into the life he now was leading. It started with a love that most around him seemed to protest. Maybe it was Dad. Dad was the one who saw the world with different eyes.

"Yeah, they did," he heard someone say. "Yeah, they did." It was the major. How did he get back in the room?

"I'm your new chief. Bright and early tomorrow. America is a resilient place." He smiled.

Mechanic's mate Samuel von Burger looked him in the eye and drew up to attention. "Yes, sir," he said.

That's what Dad would say. That's what the captain would say. That's what he would say.

He left thinking that maybe one day, his son might be good enough to compete. Maybe if he taught him well, that's what he would say in moments like these.

Not too bad a way to spend an evening.

Fuckin' A.

Chapter Twenty-Five
Morning Call

The ready room was full. The man, who was in front of them, was General Charles Yeager. He was there that day to give a pep talk to the pilots primarily, but others were in attendance. Billy was there. General Yeager was a WWII veteran, now flying B-52s. There was concern among those of rank that the pilots were missing their targets too often. The talk mixed a bit of humor with the serious nature of their business. The main point of the speech was "You are our favorite sons, make us proud. Hit the targets."

By now, Billy had been on so many missions, he'd lost track. He didn't drop bombs. But he did support and take fire. He lost a few.

The mission began routine. He was drawing fire when he realized he'd been hit.

"Billy Boy's hit," said Moray, his wing man. "I see chutes, one of them is crab tailing. Area still hot."

"Roger that, Moray, bug on it, we got a vector."

"Roger out," said Moray. He quietly said goodbye to his friend.

Chloe was looking out the living room window when she

missed a beat. A yellow taxi.

A telegram would arrive for Chloe von Burger. She was with Alicia.

"What's wrong, Mommy?" was all she heard.

Chloe could not remember what she said but remembers the distress in her daughter's eyes as she learned of the news... it was Billy. Then she wondered about Sammy. She heard her daughter run out of the room in her periphery.

"Mom?" said Sonny.

"Billy" was all she said as she held her fragile composure.

Sonny's face went ashen.

She shrugged. "He's listed as missing. Sammy's all right, as far as I know."

Sonny stood stunned, not knowing what to do. Chloe turned to him.

"Oh Sonny," she said and hugged him, holding her daughter on her leg as Alicia held on for dear life.

Chapter Twenty-Six
Jon's Purgatorium

Missing in action. What did that mean? It had been a week since receiving the news. Jon found out before he reached home. News reached him on his shift from dispatch. They called them in, and he went home.

Jon was sitting on the porch again. He didn't feel like a walk to the store for anything.

The breeze was blowing. The autumn leaves were still holding on to the trees. A slight chill in the wind, but a sunny day. The windows of the house were open. He could hear Sonny and Alicia working on her guitar skills. Those two were like peas in a pod.

"You're a natural, baby sister," said Sonny with a quaint subtle smile. Alicia never minded Sonny or Sammy calling her baby sister.

A little melancholic, she sat down her guitar.

"If you want, I'll get you up front."

She smiled. "Do you think Billy is going to be OK?"

"It takes a special magic to fly. I think special angels watch over you," said Sonny.

"Humph," she said. "Better go. Thanks for the lesson."

The window shut abruptly.

Sonny had always looked up to his older brothers. They were a tight knit bunch growing up. He didn't really cry much when he heard the news of Billy's disappearance. But he saw the hollowness of his mother's eyes. He always hoped Sammy might find a way to make things right. But Sammy was in the kitchen. He was a million miles away himself. He argued with everyone now.

He loved the Beckers, but he wondered what Sammy was thinking when he married. He spent more time here talking to Dad and Mom than he did at home. The one who seemed to be really suffering was Junior. But Junior was a good kid.

Maybe that was where there was hope. They were good kids. He sure missed Billy.

Jon's eyes misted. He wiped them, then he began to cry. What was he going to do without Billy?

His thoughts were of Sammy. *I failed him. I have failed my oldest son.* He remembered the conversations, the nun's reluctant approval, his distance, and then Chloe saved him. She saved them all.

Quietly, he blew his nose in a handkerchief. There was nowhere to hide.

Chapter Twenty-Seven
The Cookout

Bobby gave Sammy a call. It had been the end of their tour, and both of them had shipped out. It was good to be home. And it was good to hear from Bobby. At home, there was a quiet tension.

They went out to his back yard and watched their kids play. There was a small pool and a sprinkler, and they ran around in their underpants. One had a towel penned to them around their neck, like a cape.

"It won't affect my career," said Bobby. He was grilling some steaks. Both had a beer. "It will affect yours."

Sammy just looked away.

"Bonnie's been over here already, you know," said Bobby.

"Yeah, we talked about it. She said you weren't going," said Sammy.

"I said I wouldn't tell her if I was going," said Bobby. "You going?"

"You ain't saying either, I see," said Bobby. "I told them to make you a sign, so everyone would know who you were."

Sammy smiled and took a sip of his beer.

"Kind of hard to hide that," said Bobby.

"Steaks ready?" said Sammy.

"I hear you. Don't get in trouble, Sammy."

Sammy just looked at him.

"They sure are having fun, aren't they?" said Bobby. They sat down in some lawn chairs.

"Yeah, we had it made back then, didn't we?" said Sammy.

"Never better," said Bobby. "Hey, kids, you ready to eat?"

The cheerful yells of the children drowned out Sammy's melancholy. It was good to have kids.

Chapter Twenty-Eight
Protest March

Bonnie's eyes caught Sammy's. "I know what you want to do," she said. "I know what you want to do." She turned away, hands together. "And why?" Her hand went nervously to her hip.

Sammy was by the window.

"Dad says it could ruin you. It nearly ruined him."

"What do you mean?"

"He never says." She walked over to Sammy who was very stiff shouldered. He had a hard look at something out the window. She put her hand on his shoulder. He turned, and she kissed him, then turned and walked to her room.

Sammy continued to look out the window. He fell asleep in their recliner looking at the stars. Morning came too soon. And he was gone.

The drive was familiar. He rode right by Lake Michigan. He saw the place that he proposed to Bonnie, and he parked his car on the street side, near the agreed-upon rallying point. He got out of his car and walked past some empty buildings. It seemed deserted, but he heard some stirring and voices up ahead.

When Sammy walked around the corner from where he

parked, he figured this would be a defining moment. This event that was coming. He was in Chicago. He had been there many times, as a boy, and then after his tours, and now. He felt energized by what had occurred, and by his feelings toward what was going on. When he looked down the street, people were gathering. He met some friends and he had his sign. It said simply, *I went to a black school.* In bold letters. He got some chuckles from those who knew.

Bonnie was a bit disgruntled, nearly to the point of disgust with him. She even threatened to leave a time or two. Finally, they agreed to disagree. And here he was. Not the first protest rally, but one in which he was participating. He was in street clothes. When the march began, he felt he crossed a line. It wasn't long before it wasn't just them shouting. And the Chicago PD was out in force.

He heard it first, then sensed it, then tasted it. Tear gas. Someone near him was struck by something; it looked like a bottle. He then felt something hit him in the head. His reaction was instinctive. In the process, he was forced to the ground and cuffed.

He stayed there for what seemed an interminable length of time. An officer approached. He took him to a squad car and placed him in the back. By now, the fire of the protest had left him. He looked to the side as they passed the place he had been struck. Someone was covered with a sheet.

Chapter Twenty-Nine
Jail

There was a buzz, and the officer indicated to Jon he could take a seat at one of the booths for visitation. He saw his son, Sammy, enter in a bright orange jail jumpsuit. He had a black eye and a scar above his nose. He was as dissembled as he had ever seen him. He sat down.

Sammy was slow to look his dad in the eye, then finally picked up the phone.

"I know what you're going to say," Sammy finally said. "And you're right."

"Are you all right?" is what Jon finally got out. "Your mother and I have been worried."

"Where is Bonnie?" Sammy asked.

"At home with the Beckers," said Jon. "We are working on getting you out."

Sammy looked down. Then he started crying. "I was just—" he said.

"It's OK, son, it's OK. Samuel and I could tell you some stories. You know he is a Jew. We came from Germany in the 1930s."

Sammy wiped his eyes. "Yeah, I suppose so." He smiled. "I forget you and Mom were young once."

They just sat quietly for a few more minutes, then it was about time for Jon to go. "Bonnie's OK. She's got your boy. And we'll get you out soon. You're gonna do all right, son."

Sammy got up to go with the guard by his side. Jon watched him disappear through the doorway. Then he got up to go. The jail door clanged behind him.

Chapter Thirty
The Gift

It was a Gideon's Bible. Just a New Testament with the psalms added to it. The man said he would try to get him a full Bible text if he wanted. Sammy said that he would.

Sammy read it, he had nothing better to do. He read it till the covers were a bit tattered. And sang what little he remembered from church. He even learned to pray again.

One day, a year later, the man returned. He had a church pew Bible. It was worn with some use. Sammy thanked him. The man hugged him, and left. Sammy was a private man, just like his dad. He would go to church, but quietly, for prayer and supplication. He carried himself that way in the prison as well.

He sat down and opened the book up to the Proverbs. Someone had told him he should read it.

Chapter Thirty-One
The Call

The room that Sammy was ushered into was dank to say the least. It was dusty, but a ray of light warmed the place. He sat down at a table that seemed standard for such a room. It was a beat-up table of Formica with a few folding chairs. Sammy sat down and stared blankly. He looked up at the small window near the ceiling when the door opened behind him.

"Keep your seat," said a middle-aged man with a bit of a paunch. He had a tie on with a pressed shirt that was wrinkled with wear. The shirt tail was out. It was the first thing Sammy noticed as he greeted the man. He had horn-rimmed glasses and the presentable look of a detective.

"You'll be released in a few days and there are a few things I need to go over with you," he said. The man had a folder that he opened, and presented a few points of life in the free world. He felt like he was back in his unit. He listened attentively when the man placed the papers into the folder and shut it.

"Sammy, I have spoken to the colonel, and to your father—your father was in tears. I know you don't want to know that, but I am going to tell you anyway. Both these men vouched for you, and felt failure in what happened to you. So,

I'm going to give you some time to reorient to life outside these bars. And one day, I will call on you again. Then I will tell you how we clean you up the rest of the way. You won't be a stool pigeon, you are too valuable an asset to us, a far better person than that."

Sammy was looking him right in the eye now.

"Good luck to you, son." The man gathered his things and shook his hand. "We'll be in touch."

The man walked out, and the prison guard walked in. He didn't wear any cuffs. And they walked through a few secured doors that clanged as they shut to the place he had called home for nearly five years.

Chapter Thirty-Two
Camp Rainbow

The camp was called Rainbow. It was named after the rainbow found in the story of Noah, in the book of Genesis. The story told of a covenant between God and mankind. He promised never to destroy the world by flood again.

White light when separated into its component parts looks like the colors of the rainbow. There are even colors that are unseen by the human eye on the outer edges. The rainbow is formed in rain clouds, usually during a drizzle, most times after a horrible storm. It is a sign of hope.

Sammy was cleaned up, but still a bit sullen from his stay in prison. He was out, nearly free. He was as free as you could get at this point. His family brought him to a family night at the camp that Alicia frequented nearly every summer. She had taken up guitar and looked very comfortable in front of the moderately sized crowd sitting on benches set up in a wood lawn setting.

A speaker would take the makeshift podium soon. He was a younger man, dressed comfortably, but fidgeting a bit uncomfortably. As Sammy sat, he wondered what he might speak about. He didn't know the chorus that was being sung. But he did know the camp rendition of the hymn sung afterward. He knew it by heart. It was one of his father's favorites: "He walks With Me."

Then the young man took the podium as Sammy's younger sister, and the others leading the singing, sat down.

He spoke about Jonah. He began with the juniper tree and described his own personal juniper trees. He then told of the forgiving message of the Bible. He spoke of the sign of Jonah, and the early Christians that used a fish to identify one another. He asked the question, he wondered if they had any juniper trees.

Then he told about the tree at Golgotha. Some of what he talked about, Sammy knew well. Then some of what he talked about was as foreign to Sammy as Vietnam. But at the end, he smiled, a bit uncomfortably, as some said "Amen" at the end of his message.

Then from the wooden benches, the three lead singers emerged. Alicia was growing up, Sammy thought to himself. She had a flowery sun dress on. In closing, they sang the song: "Kumbaya."

The sounds of the forest were quiet, but the ever-present wind blew quietly in the trees. Almost the hush of a quiet lullaby.

Sammy looked around at the kids that were sitting there. None of them would have to go to Vietnam. Not one of them would lose their brother to a missile. They would never have to give advice to their brother to go to Canada.

An ache in his heart tugged at him, and he quietly fought off the tears that would follow.

He began to sing, "Kumbaya , my Lord." Kumbaya when translated from the Swahili means "come by here." It was a song that was said to be a favorite in West Africa, sung by the natives there. In Sammy's heart, he sang it as his pray. A prays of thanks, and a prayer of hope.

Chapter Thirty-Three
Opening Day at Disney

"How many tickets do you need?" The Disney executive had a white-collar shirt and tie. He wore some dark-rimmed glasses and looked like he could work for NASA. This was his casual attire.

"About five," said Jim.

"You have any more distant kin? This is opening day. I don't need them, neither does my family."

"I might call the von Burgers," he said.

"Next time I see you, we'll have to have lunch," said Robert. "I'll have to tell you about how we plan to use the phone lines for computers. We run all sorts of things through the phone system, you would be amazed. You still write for the newspaper?"

"Just some editorial work for the *Sanford Times*."

"I like you, Jim, you're an up and comer. Tell your family I said hello. Better get there early. And Gate B. It is all set up."

"Thanks, I will, maybe next week. Give me a call."

The call came two weeks later. They met at a PTO lunch at the local school. Both had children who attended the local elementary school. It was a school that made as much effort to be up and coming as Jim. As they walked out of the cafeteria, they watched recess. A young nine-year-old ran past and nearly ran into them.

"You're it!" said a red-headed fourth grader as she tagged another fourth grader, a boy with a crew-cut.

The playground was filled with third and fourth graders in seconds. Soon, the fifth graders would have the playground all to themselves, but for now it was filled with third and fourth graders, some climbing monkey bars, some swinging on swings, and others playing chase. Later, the fifth graders would half the crowd, but the same intensity of play.

"We could invite some of them, I suppose," said Jim.

"Probably already have," said Robert. Robert had connections to Hollywood, and Disney. He had been a projects manager overseeing the robotic productions. He told Jim that he would really enjoy 'The Hall of Presidents.'

"I've had my cooties shot!" said a tall, dark-haired fourth grader. Word was he was held back, not because of grades, but because his father had a theory that if he held his kid back a few years, he would be a star on the gridiron. No one knew how old Teddy was, except the teacher, and she knew Teddy did not want anyone to know. It was to his advantage, however, because in a game of sandlot ball, you wanted Teddy on your team. He was not only good at football, but at any game with a ball including dodge ball, baseball, and basketball. He could even play a mean soccer, and fields hockey. He did so well, some of Teddy's classmates would go home and ask their parents if they could be held back like Teddy.

There was a young black boy near Teddy. He was a live wire as well.

Jim waved back to a black lady walking out of the cafeteria. She waved back. She was Jon von Burger's daughter-in-law once removed. Jim liked her. She was an up and comer. It had been a terrible divorce. But word was the entire von Burger family was all taking it in stride. Jim, Bonnie's father well. And while a little unkempt about the whole affair, he and his were doing well.

"I think cooties shots are stupid!" said a freckled red-haired boy named Felix, who everyone knew the age of; he had been held back twice for reasons other than athletics. Once was so that his late birthday could be adjusted, the second was because he flunked reading... with a wink, Bonnie would tell you, he was an up and comer in disguise. There was something to decoding. Felix and Teddy made perfect friends when they weren't picking on or bullying smaller fourth graders.

The bell rang and interrupted the game of tag. All the participants rushed to form a line by their teacher, an older blonde-haired lady named Miss Shelia Langstrom. She liked to be called Miss Shelia though, she felt old when she was called Ms. Langstrom. She was engaged but not yet married. Her father was Jewish, but her blonde hair came from her mother. Her dad had a thing for Frauliens and Scandinavians. Her mom was his second German blonde.

"Class!" she hollered out at her kids as several other teachers organized their classes into lines to return either to their homerooms or lunch. Jimmy was glad it was lunch time.

"Michael!" cried Ms. Langstrom as Jim approached. "Samuel!"

Michael was going on a special trip to Cape Kennedy, courtesy of Bonnie's dad. Sammy was coming with him. Sammy hugged his mother and then ran to join the others.

Chapter Thirty-Four
Apollo Sunrise

Michael woke to the occasional passing of car lights on a road appropriately called A1A near Titusville.

He and his father had gotten up early. Sammy was with them. He was perking up in the back seat near the hump. They were in a blue Ford Pinto.

"Where are we, Dad?"

The darkness gave way to a check point. Jim spoke to the guard at the gate who took his pass. He handed him something that looked like a name tag.

"Just head along this road and they'll park you over by the field. They'll tell you what to do. Mrs. Becker is already waiting."

"This is near the vehicle assembly building. They are rolling out Apollo 17 this morning."

Michael's face lit up, brightening the dark car. The first hint of the sunrise was making the sky look a dark purple. Jim followed the instructions of the attendants and parked his green Ford Pinto. They followed the crowd to where a black woman and two young white men stood. Michael recognized them.

"Grandma," hollered the young black boy.

"You come here and give your grandmother a hug," said Mrs. Becker.

Junior hugged his grandmother and said a quick "Hi, Dad" to his father, Samuel.

"Hi, Jim," said Mrs. Becker. She was quite down to earth for a general's wife. To watch this event, it took some special passes. "Your wife couldn't make it."

"She left it up to us," said Jim. "She's not much for early-morning treks to the coast."

"Disney World must have worn her out," said Mrs. Becker. "You know Sammy and Sonny, don't you?"

Jim shook both their hands as they found their place. Sammy and Sonny spread a couple of quilts.

Soon, they were all sitting and munching on biscuits made by Mrs. Becker.

As the sun rose, the voices of the astronauts who were to fly their mission on the Apollo rocket gave their thoughts on the upcoming journey, and the ship that was to take them to the moon. Samuel knew one of them. He had saluted him on occasion at his duty station in Vietnam.

Slowly\, the rocket emerged from the tall rectangular black and white building. It would be the last to go to the moon.

In Chicago, Jon von Burger was arriving for his shift. Another day as an officer in the Chicago Police department, a thousand miles and a time zone away.

Chapter Thirty-Five
News

Jon was sitting in his recliner watching the five-o'clock news when the message came. He saw an Oldsmobile with a familiar faded light blue color. And the corporal who emerged from the passenger side could not have been eighteen, but he had to be at least that. There was a knock at the door and Alicia opened it.

"Dad," she said.

Jon sat down with an old Milwaukee beer on an end table. He would have a drink on his off day. He stood and walked over to the door.

"Sir," said the corporal as he saluted. He handed Jon a letter. It had an official look.

"Thank you, son," he said.

Jon waited till he had shut the door to open the letter. The contents he read twice.

"Chloe!" he shouted and ran to the back yard where Chloe was cooking dinner.

Alicia was startled as she watched her father. She could tell further that something was wrong when she saw her mother's reaction. She froze where she stood.

Then she heard her mom, "They're sure this time."

There was a hug as Jon hugged Chloe. Then Jon walked inside as Chloe sat down.

"Hun, can you come and help your mother?" he said as he poked his head inside. "Billy is alive, he's coming home."

Alicia, with some hesitance, obeyed her father, surprised at the news. She passed her father who was headed to the phone to call Sammy and Sonny. When she saw her mother, she looked worn out. Her face was ashen. But she knew her mother was happy with this news. It seemed a rather solemn occasion, the news was somehow hollow or unreal. But Alicia remembered when she received the first telegram.

"Come here, love," her mother said. And she hugged her.

After a moment, Chloe stood and picked up her glove and spatula.

"You OK, Mom?" asked Alicia.

Chloe smiled.

The air was clear, breathable. And the anxiety of waiting nearly over. They had been instructed to arrive at the airport to meet their son.

They had received the news of Billy Boy… Billy. He was coming home.

He had been identified. He was in as good health as could be expected of someone who had been a prisoner of war for five years. He would need some rehabilitation.

The news that he was returning came almost as suddenly as word that he was missing. Hardly a word about him until a few days ago.

The von Burgers were older but in good stead.

Chloe stood next to Jon. She was buried in his shoulder. Sonny was back from college; Jon had finally talked him into going. Sammy was there, standing close by, but not too close, ever vigilant. And Alicia stood with him, hand on the fence, she was looking through head held high.

The US Army prop plane rolled up the tarmac. And after what seemed an eternity, a stairwell rolled out. A door opened. Then a face, a hand, a wave. Several debarked. And then with help, Billy emerged. He had crutches.

Tears formed in Jon's eyes. This time, tears of joy. He could hear his wife make sounds of quiet joy as she left his arms to run to her boy.

Billy had come home.

Poetry from Unsung Heroes

Unsung Heroes

Not every hero
Charges down a hill
Not every patriot name is one we can recall
But every single one of them gave their very best
And gave us all their all.

It wasn't with bullets
That they sacrificed their lives
But with good deeds—and kindness
And living in a way that was right.

Oh, if necessary
They would gladly lay down their lives
They would stand in the way of infamy
To protect our way of life.

But they lived as quiet warriors
Always working behind the scenes
To make our country all that it could be
And preserve the public peace.

It was because of such sacrifice
That in being last... they became first
And helped all those around them
To overcome the worst.

But God knows their name
And everything they've done
He knows how hard they fought
And all the battles that they have won.

So, I honor them now
The unsung heroes of our world
And will continue to honor them
With my life... my deed... my word
I will show I remember them.
And try to make this a better world.

Do You Remember When?

I remember playing ball with you
You always let me win
Sometimes, I'd climb up into a tree
You'd ask about my imaginary friends.
You walked me down by the creek
You showed me where you learned to fish.
You'd tell me about the God who made the trees
And you showed me how not to sin.

You were young and strong and wise
You were my best friend...

Chorus:

Do you remember when I followed you in the snow
You always walking up ahead…
The path was made where my little feet would go
Right through the drifts and past the shed
Today, I'm still following after you
You've already made it from where you've been
Pour some coffee and wait for me
It won't be long now…
… 'Till I'll be coming home.

Do you remember when I was seventeen,
I wrecked the family car
I feared that you might yell and scream
When you saw the frame torn apart
You didn't come down too hard on me
It took all the summer wages
To repair that old car
I think I learned my lesson that day
Not to push it too hard.

You were older, gray… still wise
You were my best friend.

Chorus:

Do you remember when I followed you in the snow
You always walking up ahead…
The path was made where my little feet would go

Right through the drifts and past the shed
Today, I'm still following after you
You've already made it from where you've been
Pour some coffee and wait for me
It won't be long now...
... 'Till I'll be coming home.

I remember seeing you lying there
Your skin was cold to the touch
I knew that your soul was not there
My heart was aching so much
We said some words, sang some songs
Rode you in a special parade
To a rock garden in the town
We read a scripture
And said a prayer
We buried you in the ground...

The wind blew... and you were gone.
You were my best friend...

Bridge:

Don't you know I miss you
I have a giant hole in my heart
The tears they flow down my cheek
I just can't take being apart.

I miss you, Dad...
I'm still following you...

Chorus:
Do you remember when I followed you in the snow
You always walking up ahead...
The path was made where my little feet would go
Right through the drifts and past the shed
Today, I'm still following after you
You've already made it from where you've been
Pour some coffee and wait for me
It won't be long now...
'Till I'll be coming home...

Soon, I'm coming home...
... Oooo... I'm coming home...
... Hmmmmm...
... I'm coming home.

Oils of Arizona from AmeriKa

They say that in the harbor called Pearl
Is a white mooring
Built above a sunken boat
Inside are those
Who never saw again
Light.

They spent their last minutes tapping
Tapping on walls that were muted
To sailors
In battle exhausted from the fight
In slick waters
That were polluted

They search the darkened water
'Till dawn's early light.

They felt their efforts were futile
Though great heroism was seen
And from it a nation awoke
From its stupor and dream.

Now the oils from the depths tell the tales
Down where pearls can be made
For from the oils of the Arizona
Is a courage that has made many a sailor brave.

And in memory
Of those hidden in the depths
Flower petals fall
From maidens fair.

Remembering
Saying "Lest we forget."

And from the oils
Starting in the depths
Comes the cry with mournful sigh
"Fare thee well."